Dinner ended, but Gram wasn't done playing hostess. "Who wants fudge cake?" she asked.

Hands went up, including Mikki's. "I do, but please, can I run out to see if Popcorn will take a sugar cube from me? I'll be back before you serve dessert. I promise."

"Hurry," Brynna said. "We'll wait for you."

With a gentlemanly bow, Dad opened the door for her, then stood there, blocking it.

He froze, hands gripping the doorframe.

"Wyatt?" Gram said. "What is it?"

Even then, Sam knew she'd never forget the awful despair in her father's voice.

"Oh, Lord, phone Luke Ely and have him call out the volunteers. The bunkhouse is on fire and the flames are reaching for the barn."

*Read all the books in the* PHANTOM STALLION *series:*

# Phantom Stallion

## ∼ 3 ∼
### Dark Sunshine

TERRI FARLEY

AVON BOOKS

*An Imprint of* HarperCollins*Publishers*

Library of Congress Catalog Card Number:
2001117947
ISBN 0-06-441087-0

First Avon edition, 2002

❖

AVON TRADEMARK REG. U.S. PAT. OFF. AND IN OTHER COUNTRIES,
MARCA REGISTRADA, HECHO EN U.S.A.

Visit us on the World Wide Web!
www.harperchildrens.com

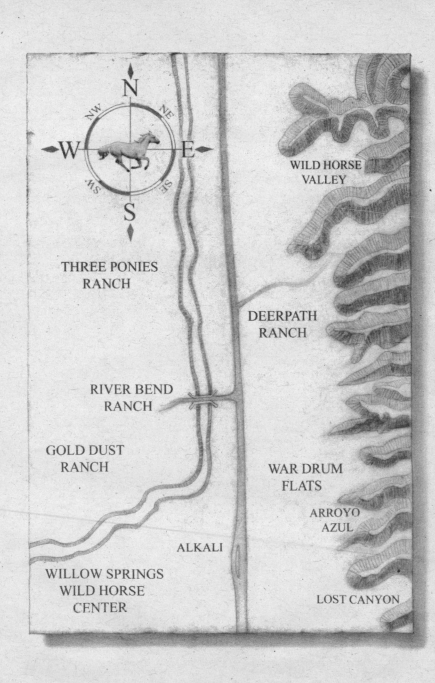

## Chapter One ᗰ

THE SWEET SMELL of horses and hay carried to Samantha Forster on an early morning breeze. She eased the front door closed behind her. Everyone inside was asleep. By rising at four o'clock, she'd beaten even Dad out of bed.

Sam stifled a yawn. She could have slept in on this September Saturday, but she and Jen planned to unlock the secrets of Lost Canyon before the sun rose.

Strange things were happening in Lost Canyon. Weird white plumes rose skyward. Were they dust, smoke, or spirits, as some Shoshone elders hinted? And what about those eerie screams?

Standing at the bus stop just the other morning, Sam and Jen had heard the faraway wails. Though they'd agreed those sounds weren't the cries of Indian ponies slaughtered there a hundred years ago, she and Jen had scared each other with other "what-ifs." They'd been rubbing gooseflesh from their arms when the school bus finally arrived.

Now, Sam moved silently across the front porch of the white, two-story house. She carried her boots and walked in stockinged feet. With Gram and Dad still sleeping, River Bend Ranch was all hers.

Darkness cloaked the neat pens and corrals, the barn and bunkhouse, and the surrounding range-lands where Hereford cattle grazed, but Sam knew it was all there waiting for her.

As she pulled on her scarred leather boots, Sam glanced toward the river. Across the current, on the wild side of the river, the Phantom could be waiting. But he'd never come to the ranch this near sunrise and probably never would.

Sam hefted her saddlebags and canteen and walked toward the barn.

Blaze woofed from his post outside the bunk-house. The border collie's bark startled a horse. Its hooves went thudding across the ten-acre pasture.

A few steps from the barn, a neigh challenged her.

"It's only me, baby," Sam whispered. She hurried. Once Ace knew it was her, he'd set up a ruckus.

Fingers flying, Sam drew the bolt on the door connecting the barn and corral. Ace followed as Sam flipped the switch for the overhead lights. The little mustang nudged Sam until he backed her against the barn wall.

"You are too sweet." She caught Ace's muzzle between her hands and gave it a quick kiss.

Sam dragged a curry comb over Ace's already glowing coat. He wasn't cross-tied or tethered, just standing with eyes half closed as he enjoyed the massaging movements of the brush.

When Sam stopped, Ace looked back over his shoulder as she smoothed on the blanket. Next, she saddled him and replaced his halter with a snaffle-bitted bridle.

Sam shivered. She should have remembered a coat. Since she hadn't, she snatched the faded green sweatshirt she kept hanging from a nail in the barn. Before pulling it on, Sam dropped Ace's reins, ground-tying him.

Like any well-schooled cow pony, Ace understood the signal to stand and wait. He snorted with impatience, though, as Sam tugged the sweatshirt over her short reddish hair.

"Sorry." Sam's muffled voice came from inside the sweatshirt.

Ace pawed the barn floor, stirring dust until she led him into the yard.

Before she could mount, Ace raised his finely boned, almost Arabic head. His nostrils flared as he gazed at the Calico Mountains, where a rim of midnight blue showed above the peaks.

Sam swung into the saddle.

"Don't get your hopes up," she told the horse. "We're heading away from his territory."

Sam shifted her weight slightly. Ace started

toward the bridge, answering her cue.

"No reason to think we'll see him, boy," she said, but Sam had watched wild horses travel the trail into Lost Canyon.

Once, they'd been led by the Phantom.

Jen and her high-stepping palomino weren't at the pond by War Drum Flats. Although she was disappointed, Sam could guess why.

All week Jen had sniffled and sneezed, but she'd carried a backpack full of tissues and refused to miss a single day of classes. Sam would bet the flu had finally gotten the better of her friend.

She was out here alone.

Then she heard it. The weird warbling was impossible to identify until it changed to a piercing cry.

Ace trembled. Through the saddle leather and blanket, Sam felt him, and knew the cry was no cougar's scream. It was the plea of a terrified horse.

Sam wheeled Ace away from the pond and aimed him toward the tumble of boulders and sagebrush leading toward the path. The gelding moved at a stiff-legged trot.

"I know you don't want to go, but that horse is in trouble." Sam knew Lost Canyon lay someplace between here and that highest peak wearing a cap of snow. "C'mon, Ace. I'd want someone to help if you were crying."

Ace moved into a grudging lope, but the steep

uphill path meant he couldn't maintain the pace for long. Just when the footing grew more level, the trail dead-ended into a rock wall. Water seeped from a crack running across its face.

They backtracked until the path turned into a deer trail. Sam almost lost it on a slick stretch of granite.

Sam slowed Ace, stroked his coarse black mane, and listened. She hadn't heard the whinny for several minutes. When she closed her eyes to concentrate, she did hear something. It was a whirring motor, like a chain saw. This high up the mountain, the sound could have carried from anywhere.

"Just a little farther," Sam told Ace.

The gelding picked his way across the rock, then grunted with irritation as Sam urged him onto a narrow ledge.

Ace did as she asked, but he clearly disagreed. The little mustang understood searching for grass and water. He understood people expected him to chase calves. But running toward a place where one horse was *already* in trouble? Ace shook his mane in disgust.

Suddenly the ground turned bare and sandy. Something was wrong. A thick stand of juniper lay ahead. Nothing should have rubbed this rugged terrain bare of vegetation.

Sam wished the sun would hurry and rise. The buzzing sound drew closer, but she still couldn't see its source. Ace looked back, and Sam heard the sound of galloping hooves.

"You're right, boy. We're out of here." Sam searched the area and spotted an outcropping of rock. She slid to the ground, jogged toward the rock. Ace followed.

The juniper branches were bare on the side facing the trail, as if something had rubbed the leaves off. Sam had just seconds to hide behind the rock before a buckskin horse exploded onto the trail.

Black forelock blowing back from a golden face, the mustang ran, widemouthed and foaming, eyes rolled white with terror. Her delicate legs pulled her away from the noise, toward the path that narrowed like a funnel into the juniper just ahead.

As the horse passed, Sam saw a red bandanna knotted around the mare's throat.

A trap! Sam knew it an instant before she saw the shambling horses that followed the buckskin. The panicky buckskin was a Judas horse, leading the others into a trap. Necks dark with sweat, the mustangs veered too close to the trail's crumbling edge. One more step would send them plummeting to their deaths.

But the mustangs ran on, fleeing the buzz of motorcycles ridden by men in straw cowboy hats. There were two of them.

The men whooped and yipped over the whining motorcycles. Horses crashed into each other, into boulders. They feared the men and machines more than the trap.

A dun with tiger-striped forelegs vaulted up a steep path just past the spot where Sam and Ace were hiding. The path went nowhere. As the mare wheeled and slid back down the path in a shower of rocks, Sam recognized her as the Phantom's lead mare.

Sam covered her mouth. No, no. Just weeks ago, the Phantom had been turned loose by the Bureau of Land Management. He was protected, freed to run wild and strengthen the mustang breed. How could he do that if BLM took his herd off the range?

If she burst out now, the horses would shy off the hillside. The fall might break their legs or necks. She had to wait until they were safely corralled. But this didn't look anything like the government gathers she'd heard about. It was too rough and primitive, too risky for horses the BLM was supposed to protect.

As one of the vehicles roared past, Sam realized it wasn't a dirt bike but an all-terrain vehicle. It was driven by a man in a shirt that looked like army camouflage. Attached to the vehicle was a scabbard holding a rifle.

These whooping idiots didn't work for the BLM. They were wild horse rustlers.

Ace lifted his head. Before he could neigh, Sam grabbed his muzzle and pulled it down. She pressed her cheek against the gelding's.

"You have to be quiet, boy," she whispered. "They're criminals."

Men committing a federal crime wouldn't mind

hurting the only witness to their wrongdoing. Sam swallowed hard. If something happened to her, Dad and Gram might assume she'd suffered another riding accident. They might never know the truth.

A sleek black yearling flashed before Sam. A pair of blood bay mares followed. This was definitely the Phantom's herd. How could she save them?

Ahead, inside the trap, the buckskin lowered her head to a bucket so full of grain it spilled over at the thrust of her nose. The mare bolted the food in desperate gulps, ribs working like bellows. The men had starved her. That's how they'd forced the mare to lead the others into the trap.

She was so hungry, she ignored the chaos at the mouth of the trap. Inspired by the attempted escape of the tiger dun, other horses circled away from the ropes that had been strung on each side of the path and camouflaged with khaki-colored garbage bags. If the horses continued down the path, they'd be hemmed in on both sides and funneled into a pen made of metal panels so tall that there was no chance they could leap to freedom.

Sam saw the trap clearly now. So did the horses, but they had no place else to go. The tiger dun wouldn't let them enter, but she didn't know where to lead.

Movement beyond the trap made Sam spot a third man, on a horse. He raised his arm and pointed. For an icy moment, Sam feared he'd spotted her, but then the horseman shouted.

"He's mine!"

Even before she looked, Sam knew. And then the Phantom burst into the clearing.

Thick-muscled and furious, the Phantom shone silver amid the whirlwind of dust. Head held flat on a lowered neck, he slashed the rump of a roan mare, driving her away from the trap, toward a downhill path so steep it seemed to plunge into space.

Swinging his head, the Phantom herded another mare after the roan. When she trotted in place, hesitating, the stallion's teeth convinced her to run.

Like a striking snake, the silver stallion worked his way through the herd, bullying his family away from the trap that would end their freedom.

"Stop him! They're all getting away!"

"Hey, close the gate!"

The buzzing vehicles only made the herd flee faster. Hooves clattered on rock, and the sounds of falling horses told Sam the descent down the Phantom's escape trail wasn't easy.

The horseman trotted forward, swinging a lazy loop of rope above his head.

Oh, no. He wanted to rope the Phantom.

The stallion hated ropes and feared them. The scar on his neck told why. With a choice between the rope and the cliff, the stallion would leap and die.

The buckskin shied from the horseman. With a metallic banging, she hit the side of the portable corral disguised with juniper. She feared the rope but kept her head down, eating in the midst of chaos as if nothing else mattered.

Only a few horses still milled inside the corral, near the buckskin: an old bay mare, a bald-faced roan, the black yearling, and a chestnut colt. Not enough to sacrifice the herd for, and yet the Phantom stayed.

*Run. Go now!* Sam sent her thought to the stallion as she had before, but he wouldn't leave the others behind.

The loop flew, closed on air, and slapped the stallion's back. The rider swore and jerked the rope away for a second try.

*Run, boy, run.*

Before the rider threw another loop, the Phantom darted inside the trap.

"Close the gate!"

Sam's leg muscles tensed. She was ready to sprint from cover, ready to launch herself at the man dismounting from the ATV, but the Phantom had noticed. He was wheeling, herding the colt before him.

*Just wait*, Sam told herself. *He can do it. He can make it.*

The man in camouflage was closing the gate, but the stallion charged, knocking the man aside.

Falling, the man reached up, as if he could grab the Phantom's mane. The chestnut youngster ran on, but the stallion stopped. His head turned, ears flattened to his neck and eyes narrowed. The man saw what he was risking and stumbled out of range of the Phantom's flashing teeth.

With a whisk of his tail, the stallion leaped after his herd and vanished.

Ace's breath sighed against Sam's cheek. The horse was as relieved as she, but only one danger had ended.

## Chapter Two ⌒

S AM SQUATTED and hid. She wished the juniper foliage was more dense. She wished daybreak hadn't come while the rustlers battled the Phantom for his herd.

The three horses left behind didn't provide much of a distraction. Sooner or later, the men would see her.

The black yearling trotted a stride ahead of the bay mare and the stocky roan. Together, they formed a small herd and circled the pen made of portable steel panels. The buckskin shone like a spot of sunlight among the darker horses, but each time they reached her, the three horses veered aside. Just the same, the buckskin always kicked out a rear hoof in warning.

The mustangs showed no interest in her grain. They ran as if they could escape their captivity, and stopped only once, calling after the others as if their wild hearts would break.

Sam grabbed Ace's muzzle when his nostrils vibrated in response. He yanked his head from her grasp. For a minute, Sam felt a cold clutch of dread, but the gelding stayed quiet.

"Well, shoot, this wasn't hardly worth the trouble," said one man. He climbed off his dirt bike, then snatched off his straw hat and swatted it against his pant leg.

Though Sam had seen her father make the same gesture a hundred times, on this man it looked wrong. He wasn't a cowboy, just a man dressed up like one.

"Old mare's so bony, don't think she'll weigh up to a hundred bucks," said the man, and because his wide, freckled face looked good-natured, Sam disliked him even more.

Still mounted, the rider wrapped his rope into a neat coil as he spoke. "What we lose on the old one, we'll make up with the roan. Get 'em loaded. I'll be back."

As he rode away, Sam wondered where he could be going. More than that, she wondered what the men were talking about.

*Weigh up to a hundred bucks?*

Sam tried to make sense of the conversation. But when the man in camouflage pulled a rifle, her brain could only focus on it. She had to stay hidden. She must keep Ace silent and still.

Sam tried to get a good look at the men. If the police caught them later, she wanted to be able to identify them. It was difficult from where she was hiding. The man in camouflage had a broad and freckled face. The man who'd snatched off his hat had bushy white hair and eyes that bulged.

Before she had a chance to focus on the last guy, the men began tugging at the edge of a huge sort of blanket. It looked like a patchwork quilt made of feed sacks. As they pulled it away, Sam saw they'd used it to cover a small stock truck.

A sigh shuddered through Sam, but the men were too busy to notice. The feed sack quilt made a great disguise. She'd been staring at the hidden truck for at least twenty minutes, but she hadn't noticed it. From the air, it would look like part of the rough terrain. From below, it blended with the rock and juniper.

Although the Ford truck was a fairly new model, it was painted a muddy yellow that didn't shine, even in full sunlight. Hitched on behind was a gray stock trailer. An orange stripe, probably reflective, had been painted on its side. It was big enough to carry at least a dozen animals.

Sam didn't know how they'd driven the truck up the mountain or how they'd get it back down again, but the men set to work with an ease indicating they'd done this many times before.

How many horses had they kidnapped off the range, and where had they taken them?

Sam didn't know the man on the horse had

returned until he climbed into the pen with the mustangs. He moved like a cowboy, but he must be a crazy one.

Quickly, she saw he had nothing to fear. With each step he took, the frightened horses scattered.

He carried a thick-handled black bullwhip. Seeing this, the buckskin left her food and joined the other horses. Her shrill neighing began. Sam recognized it as the sound that had floated down the mountain as she and Jen had waited for the bus yesterday.

This close, the piercing sound hardly seemed equine.

Mustangs were usually silent, and the BLM freeze brand on her neck proved the buckskin was a mustang. But someone had taught her to scream.

The men on the outside dropped one panel of the corral. All four horses bolted for the opening. When they saw they were stampeding toward the truck ramp, they shied and turned back. But the man with the whip left them no choice.

The lash snaked outward, popping in their faces. The mustangs stopped, sliding back on their haunches, then wheeled toward the ramp.

That quickly, the animals were conquered. Heads low, their mouths made submissive chewing movements. In the language of wild horses, they begged for mercy.

The man only cracked his whip again.

Although frightened by the hollow pounding of their hooves on the ramp, the horses went. They didn't know what lay before them, but they fled the whip.

The buckskin was last. Her legs and body trembled so much, Sam feared she would collapse.

Gathering her courage, the buckskin leaped toward the ramp. As she did, the man in camouflage got a foothold on the metal fence, swung up, and leaned toward her. Before the buckskin could swerve away, he grabbed at the red bandanna around her neck and tugged it up to cover her eyes.

She stopped, standing still as the man laughed.

"She done it again," he said, laughing. "Never quite figures out she's not goin' with 'em, does she?"

His cruelty almost made Sam burst from her hiding place. Now she understood. The buckskin mare had been starved and used to lure wild mustangs into this trap many times before.

Each time the wild ones were loaded into the truck, the buckskin thought she'd escape. Each time, she was left behind in darkness.

Sam swallowed hard, making the mare a silent promise. As soon as the men left, she'd free her.

The man in camouflage stowed the rifle on a gun rack inside the truck cab. That made Sam's determination more solid. She'd been quick and agile when she played basketball for her middle school team.

Without that gun to fear, she could outmaneuver those men and release the buckskin.

Yes, she might be stealing, but Sam didn't care. She'd just figured out where the rustlers took the wild horses.

Only one kind of business purchased mustangs by the pound—the kind that made them into horse meat.

The mud-yellow truck swayed from side to side, gears grinding, engine laboring. The horses inside couldn't possibly stay on their feet. The truck's engine made a weird pinging sound as it slogged down the back side of the mountain, safe from eyes that might have seen it go down the front side, toward the highway.

Though Sam had watched all three men climb into the truck, she still didn't move. Where was the horse the cowboy had ridden? Where had he gotten that whip? Was someone else still around?

She could climb back on Ace and ride fast, back the way she'd come. She glanced at her watch and was amazed to see it was only seven o'clock. She could get home and report the men to Brynna Olson at the BLM and still save the mare.

Unless they delivered the horses to someone nearby and returned to collect the abused buckskin who did her job so well.

· Sam had started to sip from her canteen when she noticed the buckskin had no water. The corral was empty of anything but the plastic grain bucket.

"That does it," she muttered to Ace. "You've got a new friend, boy."

After all the commotion, it wouldn't be fair to trust Ace to ground-tying. If he had any sense at all, he'd head for home. And she couldn't let him. Sam knotted the reins around a thick piece of brush, then surveyed the area one last time. Nothing moved except the buckskin mare.

"Things could get a little weird, Ace," Sam whispered. "If they do, just think like a mustang, okay?"

She gave Ace a final pat and started toward the corral. Sam walked boldly, wondering how fast she could run back, untie Ace, vault onto his back, and escape if anyone hollered "Stop!"

The buckskin's ears were a beautiful dark gold edged in black, and they swiveled to catch each one of Sam's steps.

Sam paused outside the gate. The man who'd pulled the bandanna up to cover the mare's eyes had done it with little fuss. Sam thought she could probably pull it down, except that the mare wasn't anywhere near the fence.

The bolt on the fence clanged back. If anyone was around, he would come charging out now. Sam held her breath and listened. A shadow surprised her, until she realized it was a hawk sailing on updrafts around the snowy peak.

She left the gate ajar. Running in boots was next to impossible, but if someone appeared, she'd try sprinting back to Ace. She'd trust her life to his speed and surefootedness.

She should have been worrying about the mare.

Black forelegs thrashed through the air as the mare leaped toward Sam.

*Like a cougar.* The words flashed through Sam's mind as she flung herself left, out of the buckskin's path, and rolled in the dirt. Instinctively, her arms came up, shielding her head as the buckskin came even with her. Sam's eyes were clamped shut, awaiting that awful slam of hooves on skull.

Darkness closed around her like a swarm of bees, but Sam didn't pass out and the buckskin's kick never came.

As the buckskin's hooves retreated, Sam rolled and regained her feet. The buckskin was still blindfolded, but free.

Sam worried as she jogged back to Ace. The trail to the top had been a challenge with her eyes and Ace's working overtime. How could the buckskin stampede down the hill sightless?

Breathing hard, Sam stabbed her thumb on the juniper as she jerked Ace's reins loose. She glanced up to see the buckskin picking her way across the slick granite. Then she started down the twisting trail.

Instinct had kept the buckskin from following the scent of the Phantom's herd over the cliff, but did she know where she was going?

Sam swung into the saddle. The gelding was eager, but with the buckskin just ahead of her, Sam kept Ace reined in.

"Easy, boy," Sam said, leaning close to his neck. "You're going to have to help me do this."

They followed the mare at a distance, until she stopped at the wide spot in the trail where water seeped from a crack in the rock. Sam remembered this spot. They were almost down.

Still blindfolded, the mare lapped at the moisture.

Sam watched and waited, giving the buckskin a chance to drink.

The mare was tiny, thirteen hands or a little taller. Her black mane tangled down to her shoulder. Her ribs stood out with hollows in between.

Ace nickered, and there was something excited and hopeful in the way the little mare turned to him. She risked a step in his direction, slipped on hooves that hadn't been trimmed in a long time, then took one more step and returned his inquiring nicker.

*That's it*, Sam thought. She trusts Ace.

Sam remembered Brynna's tale of her blind mustang, Penny, who followed her rider's cues out of trust. And Sam remembered the Phantom, galloping down a hillside in the dark beside Ace, out of trust.

Sam would stay silent. Scary as it was, she'd leave the red blindfold in place and hope the mare followed Ace all the way home.

Sam kept her eyes on the horizon, on clouds like dandelion fluff against the blue sky. She didn't glance toward the buckskin for fear the mare would sense it.

When Sam heard the rushing river and saw the soaring wood rectangle that marked the entrance to River Bend Ranch, she knew they'd reached the final tests.

The mare would hear her hooves clack on the wooden bridge. She'd scent strange horses and humans.

And Sam had her own test to pass: Dad.

In the months since she'd been home, Sam had hinted, suggested, and implied that she wanted to adopt another mustang. Each time, Dad refused. Animals needed to earn their feed, he insisted.

Sam thought of Strawberry, Banjo, Ace, and Tank, just a few of River Bend's sensible, hardworking cow ponies. Then she thought of the buckskin. Even filled with expensive feed, she might remain skittish and nervy. But one thing weighed in the mare's favor: Dad wouldn't have been able to leave her behind, either.

For nearly an hour now, the buckskin had followed Ace. He seemed to understand his responsibility. If the mare lagged behind, Ace shortened his stride. If she kept pace a quarter mile to the gelding's right, Ace's ears swiveled in her direction. Once, she'd come so close that her skeletal barrel had bumped Sam's stirrup.

Sympathy had welled up in Sam, but she stayed quiet. Words wouldn't comfort a horse who'd received only pain from humans.

*Almost there*, she thought. *Little horse, you're almost safe.*

Gram must have glimpsed them from the kitchen window, because she was standing on the front porch as they rode up. A breeze blew Gram's denim skirt against her legs and picked at the gray hair pinned into a tidy bun. She wiped her hands on her blue apron, watching Sam, Ace, and the buckskin clatter over the bridge and into the ranch yard.

Gram smiled, and Sam knew that look on her face. Gram was wishing she could tell Mom all about it. Even though Sam's mom was dead, Gram said she talked to her daughter-in-law in prayers, every night.

The buckskin hesitated when a tide of horses gathered at the fence of the ten-acre pasture. The sound of those hooves, without being able to see if the other horses were welcoming or rejecting her, must have frightened the mare. But she stayed next to Ace until he stopped near the round corral.

Jake was inside gentling a horse for a neighbor, but the gate hinges squeaked. Any second now, Jake would appear, wondering what she'd done this time.

Jake was sixteen, older than Sam by three years. Right now, he looked even older. Shoshone black hair tied back with a leather thong, fringed chinks buckled over his jeans, Jake took in all there was to know in a single glance.

Raising his brown eyes to Sam's, he nodded, assuring her that he wouldn't frighten the mare by speaking.

He didn't, until she'd ridden Ace to the barn, stripped him of saddle and bridle, and turned both horses into the barn corral with Gram's gentle paint, Sweetheart.

Exhausted and finally drinking from her canteen, Sam watched the buckskin. Clearly, she was familiar with corrals. She didn't fling herself against the rails as some wild ones did.

Still blindfolded, the mare stood sandwiched between Ace and Sweetheart. Heedless of the hot day, the buckskin let the two horses press against her. At last, she dozed in the security of her new herd.

As Sam walked back toward the house, Jake met her halfway. She almost wished he hadn't. He wore the same lazy tomcat smile he'd taunted her with when she was a tagalong kid.

"What?" she demanded.

"Brat," Jake began.

"Stop calling me that. And stop laughing."

Sam tilted her canteen to take a long drink of water.

Once her mouth was full, Jake continued.

"I just can't wait to hear what Wyatt says when he finds out his daughter is a for-real horse thief."

## Chapter Three ⌘

"**I**'M NOT A horse thief!"

"Um-hmm," Jake said. "That freeze brand and bandanna probably don't mean a thing. Her owner just gave her to you."

"No," Sam admitted. "But I didn't steal her. Exactly. If you'd seen what they were doing to her—"

"The owner was right there?" Jake's brown eyes widened. "You mean we're not talking burglary but outright robbery?"

"Of course not," Sam said, but she wasn't sure. "I just, well, there was nothing else I could do."

"Tell it to the judge." Jake turned back toward the round corral.

"Hey!" Frustrated, Sam gave Jake's retreating back a flat-handed push. "You can't just walk away."

"Bet me," Jake said, and kept walking.

"If you opened your eyes and looked at her, you'd see that mare is starved, dehydrated, and—" Sam searched for words to explain the horse's terror. "And she's an emotional mess."

When he turned back around, Jake's face was shadowed by his black Stetson. "I'll help you get that rag off her head," Jake said, but Sam could tell his sympathies were for the horse, not her.

"I don't want your help," Sam blurted. "I want you to admit I didn't steal that mare. I rescued her."

"Whatever," Jake muttered. His spurs rang as he led the way back to the barn corral.

"You hate it when I'm right," Sam taunted, but Jake didn't reply. Sometimes she thought he had a daily quota of words, and when they were used up, he just quit talking.

Jake approached the buckskin cautiously, coming through the shady barn to the corral. Sam blinked, letting her eyes adjust to the dimness, but Jake wasted no time. He set one boot on a fence rail, pushed himself up, and reached for the buckskin's head.

The mare exploded. Her piercing scream accompanied an attack. She went for Jake with such fury that one foreleg got hung by the knee over the top rail.

"It's okay, girl. It's okay," Sam heard herself babbling, but Jake stayed quiet, dodging the mare's teeth as he freed her leg, then jumped down.

Jake would only snap at her if she asked if he was okay, so Sam watched the horse instead.

The buckskin ricocheted around the corral. She slammed against the fence, banged into Ace, bumped Sweetheart, then collided with the fence again.

The mare had been calm and napping just minutes ago. Sam could see it wasn't captivity the buckskin feared, it was people.

Jake motioned Sam outside the barn, but he kept staring back toward the mare, trying to read her mind.

"I'm calling Brynna Olson," Sam said. Jake nodded, eyes still on the horse. "To see who adopted her and everything. And—"

Sam's heart sped up. How could she have put aside the safety of the other horses? "I'll ask her where someone would take mustangs to sell them for—" She couldn't swallow down the worry. "You know, to be made into dog food."

"They'd take them out to the auction yards in Mineral," Jake said. "But there's a brand inspector there. If he thinks the horses are mustangs, he won't let them go up for sale."

"Are you sure?" Sam thought of the two mares and the beautiful black yearling.

"Yeah." Jake sounded bored, but Sam could see he was just preoccupied, still staring at the buckskin. "When you get done, come back."

"Why?" She'd had every intention of doing just that, but Sam didn't like Jake bossing her around.

"She might let you take that blindfold off," he said.

Sam felt dizzy, remembering the mare's charge on the mountain, remembering she'd almost fainted from fear. But Jake never suggested she do something dangerous.

"Piece of cake," Sam said, then hurried off to make that phone call, half hoping Gram would forbid her to leave the house.

"I'll dispatch two rangers the minute we hang up. One can check out the auction yards. The other can go up by Lost Canyon and determine who's responsible." Brynna Olson, director of Willow Springs Wild Horse Center, sounded crisp and businesslike.

She always did. Sam still had to look hard to see the kind woman inside that wrinkle-free government uniform.

Still, Brynna was awfully good at her work. With a few questions, she'd pried a lot of information from Sam's weary brain. Now, Sam could clearly picture the three men: the freckle-faced one in camouflage, the white-haired one with the buggy eyes, and the cowboy who'd flicked the black whip with such easy cruelty.

The buckskin's screams invaded the kitchen. Gram, who'd been sipping coffee and listening to Sam's conversation, frowned.

"I'll read that location back to you," Brynna said. "Correct anything I might've taken down incorrectly."

Brynna read Sam's description of the trail into Lost Canyon. Of course, she'd copied it perfectly.

"You've got it," Sam said, trying to block out the commotion coming from the barn pen.

"This evening when I drive out to talk with Wyatt," Brynna said, "I'll check the mare's freeze mark and start tracking her owner. What else should I know?"

Sam bit her lip. So far, she hadn't mentioned the Phantom or said it had been his herd driven toward the trap. The less folks thought about the stallion, the better. It couldn't possibly matter.

"They were using her as a Judas horse," Sam blurted. "They must have turned her loose farther down the mountain, then spooked the mustangs after her. She led them right into the trap, as if she knew there'd be food there. She's half starved and dehydrated."

"I'll send a vet."

Suddenly there was a ringing thump outside, as if the mare were trying to kick her way out of the barn corral.

"Send a big one," Sam said. "She's a fighter."

It turned out Sam didn't have to remove the buckskin's blindfold. Sweetheart rubbed faces with her and accidentally peeled off the bandanna, and that's when the mare had gone crazy all over again.

"She's fine as long as she faces that way." Jake

pointed. He'd been watching her the whole time Sam was on the phone. "Looking into the dark barn, she's fine. She started coming unglued when I turned on the light to get a look at her."

Was something wrong with the buckskin's eyes? Sam had assumed the men had blindfolded the mare to make her helpless, but maybe she was extra sensitive to light. Sam knew nothing about horses' eyes, and she had no time to ask Jake before she heard riders approaching.

Dad and all three cowboys—Dallas, Pepper, and Ross—were crossing the bridge. They rode loose-jointed and tired, like men who'd already put in a full day's work.

Sam looked at her watch. She could hardly believe it was already 4 P.M. She swallowed against the tension threatening to strangle her, but then she saw her calf, Buddy, frolic up to the gate to greet the riders. Ever since she'd been pulled from quicksand as an orphan, the calf had been peppy as a pup.

Dad stripped the saddle and bridle from Banjo and turned the horse into the big pasture. While he rinsed his hands and face at the pump, Sam remembered she hadn't brushed her hair since dawn, when she had pulled her ratty green sweatshirt over her head.

She forked fingers through her bangs and the tendrils at her temples, trying to fluff the hair flattened by her old brown cowboy hat.

Now, saddle and blanket in hand, Dad walked toward the tack room.

"Steady there." Jake's voice was so low only the horses heard, but he was talking to Sam. "The worst thing that can happen is we give the mare to BLM."

Jake was right, but Sam noticed he hadn't ridden home for dinner. Suspense had its claws in him, too. He wanted to hear what Dad and Brynna said about this frightened animal.

"What do we have here?" Dad asked.

Sam listened for judgment in his voice, but heard only curiosity about the golden tan mare who refused to look at him.

As Sam began to explain, Brynna arrived. So did the vet. Gram walked down from the house, too, and all three cowboys put off dinner to see what was causing the excitement.

Sam supposed she did a fine job of explaining. After all, no one could contradict her except Ace or the rustlers, and one seemed as likely as the other. But Sam was distracted.

Not by Dad, who stood expressionless as a tree trunk. Not by Brynna, who took notes like a newspaper reporter. Sam wasn't distracted by the vet, who said he wouldn't sedate the mare for an exam now, since he'd have to tranquilize her again tomorrow when BLM moved her to Willow Springs.

Sam was distracted by the girl who'd arrived with Brynna. The BLM woman was so caught up in identifying the mare, she'd forgotten to introduce the girl who'd come in the white government truck along with her.

The girl had a pointy fox face and wispy blond hair, and though she couldn't be more than twelve years old, she was what Aunt Sue would call a "tough cookie." Hands on hips, eyelids slack with boredom, she looked at those around her—Sam included—as if they were barely smart enough to breathe.

The vet had to detour around the girl to leave. She wouldn't step out of his path. Only Sam seemed to notice.

Was the girl Brynna's daughter? Her niece? If so, Sam pitied Brynna. The girl looked mean. Her jaw jutted out as if she held a grudge against the world.

"I think they kept her in a dark stall, long-term," Jake suggested.

A flicker of fear lit the girl's face before she gave a forced and noisy yawn.

"It happens," Brynna said. She gave the girl a quick glance, but gestured toward the horse. "Even a mustang gets to feeling safe when she's left undisturbed. Then, when they try to make her leave, she charges."

"Yes, she does." Sam could have kicked herself for saying it.

Dad and Gram turned frowns her way. Their expressions said that the hours they'd spent at her hospital bedside, two years ago, were still fresh in their memories.

"When I opened the gate up there, she ran for it." Sam gestured toward Lost Canyon, then made things worse by brushing off the front of her jeans. "I fell getting out of her way."

Figuring the girl would be amused by her discomfort, Sam shot her a sidelong glance. She was wrong.

The girl wasn't listening to a word she'd said. She was watching the horses.

In the ten-acre pasture, Strawberry rolled the saddle stiffness from her back, then shot to her feet and ran with the others galloping after. It happened every evening, but you couldn't guess that by the girl's expression. For the first time, Sam thought she was seeing rapture.

If the little creep loved horses, she couldn't be all bad.

Just then, Jake leaned forward to show Brynna the bandanna the buckskin had worn, and he accidentally bumped the girl.

"Sorry," Jake apologized.

Instead of shrugging off the encounter, the girl stepped closer, lifted her chin and shot both hands out to her sides, fingers motioning him closer.

Sam blinked. The girl was clearly saying that if Jake wanted to fight, she was ready.

Jake looked stunned. Sam watched him calculate the huge difference in their heights and weights, but he only repeated, "Sorry."

Sam glanced at Dad to gauge his reaction to all this, and caught him looking at Brynna. Something in the tilt of Dad's head said they'd already discussed this kid. Their eyes continued the conversation and Sam felt left out.

"I forgot to introduce Mikki," Brynna said.

"Mikki," Gram repeated. "What a cute name."

Gram stepped forward to take the girl's hand in both of hers, but Mikki crossed her arms and cinched them close to her body.

Sam couldn't believe someone didn't tell the girl to straighten up and apologize.

"Mikki is from Sacramento, California," Brynna went on. "She goes by Mikki, but her full name is Michelle Small."

The girl glared at Sam as if daring her to comment on the match between her name and her size.

"Mikki's agreed to be the first to try out the HARP program—that's the Horse and Rider Protection program—here in northern Nevada," Brynna said.

Sam felt her lips twist in sarcasm. With Mikki's attitude, people needed protection *from* her.

"Some people who adopt mustangs just aren't suited to the chore of training them. Sometimes, they make some pretty big mistakes," Brynna said. "When that happens, we take the horses back and match them with girls who gentle them and make them adoptable all over again."

Sam would have asked Brynna how they picked the girls, if Jake hadn't chosen that moment to escape.

"'Scuse me," he mumbled. "I'm due home soon, and it'll take a while to finish up with Teddy and turn him out."

Dad glanced toward the round corral where Jake had left the horse he was working, then nodded for Jake to go ahead.

"Bye, Jake," Sam said. She waved, and watched Dallas, Pepper, and Ross go after him. Cowboys didn't willingly join in uncomfortable conversations. Sam was amazed Dad was still standing here.

"Teddy Bear is the nicest little horse," Gram explained. "He's a curly Bashkir. Maybe you've seen them in magazines."

When Gram added that, Sam realized why she'd gone off on this tangent. Once more, Mikki's face lit with that joyous look. Even though Mikki had been rude, Gram was entertaining her. Why?

"Jake's schooling Teddy for Mr. Martinez, a banker in town. He loves that horse, but he raised him from a baby and, well, spoiled him a bit. Some tricks that were cute when Teddy was a colt—like using his teeth to pull the wallet out of your back pocket—are downright dangerous now that he's an adult horse. And when he doesn't want to be ridden?" Gram raised her eyebrows. "He just sits down like a big old dog."

When Brynna noticed Mikki's smile, her own got bigger. "Mikki, why don't you go over and watch?"

Even Sam knew the girl wouldn't take the bait. Brynna had a lot to learn about kids.

"So you can talk behind my back? It's not like I can't guess what you're going to say." Mikki slung her thumbs in her jeans pockets before facing Sam's father. "Here's the deal, *sir*." She made the word an insult. "HARP can't place me in the California program because of my juvenile record, my *crimes*, got it?"

Mikki's head wagged a little as she talked. Her tone was sarcastic, as though trying to shock Wyatt Forster was fun.

"Shoplifting, fighting, runaway." Mikki ticked her offenses off on three fingers. "What Ms. Olson didn't say is that HARP matches *at-risk* girls with wild horses who've been messed up."

Sam almost nodded, and Mikki turned to her.

"Yeah, and I'm past 'at-risk.' Everyone in the state of California has given up on me. Even my mom. She's the one who sent me to this freaking desert—"

When Mikki stopped, Brynna took over without a hint of emotion.

"Mikki is living in a group home in Darton. Although she's just eleven, she's in a program for academically talented students and she's going to middle school there," Brynna explained. "The situation's not as bleak as she says. HARP is a very popular program in California, and it's just getting started in Nevada."

"Look." Mikki's hands perched on her hips. She turned her back on Gram and Dad to face Brynna. "This perfect little family doesn't want me around. Can't you tell? And I really don't care. I only said I'd do this because I sort of like horses."

Mikki gave a snort. Then, carefully not glancing toward Teddy as Jake led him prancing to the pasture, Mikki walked to the white BLM truck, climbed in, and slammed the door.

As soon as the kid disappeared, Brynna started talking fast.

"River Bend Ranch is the perfect place to start HARP in Nevada. You've got the round corral for starting the mustangs and girls together. And once you get the rails up on that big pasture near the barn, it will work for an arena, when they start riding. As I've, uh, explained, before." Brynna hesitated.

The BLM woman looked from Gram, who looked excited by the idea, to Dad. His face was blank, not giving Brynna a flicker of encouragement. But she kept talking.

"And, of course, the big bunkhouse would be perfect."

*For what?* Sam wondered.

Brynna pointed to a weathered building with

broken windowpanes and a roof buckled at the peak and stripped bare of shingles by the wind. Cowboys hadn't slept there for years. Sam had heard Dallas say it was home to spiders big as lions and he wouldn't go in there without a whip and a chair.

Gram must have been thinking the same thing. When Brynna saw Gram frown, she added, "It will take some fixing up, but HARP, as I've said before"—she glanced at Dad—"pays ranchers for hosting the program if the pilot program succeeds."

Brynna took a breath before she went on.

"And the girls would do so much better here than at the Gold Dust. Mr. Slocum's volunteered, but Sam would be a far better influence than—" Brynna gestured in the general direction of Linc Slocum's ranch, and Sam mentally filled in the blank.

*Rachel.* The most popular girl at Darton High School, Rachel Slocum was beautiful, catty, and selfish. Her rich father gave her whatever she wanted. Rachel was bored by horses, and she'd scorn girls who had the bad luck not to be born wealthy and pretty.

Sam knew *that* from experience.

But wait. Sam reined in her dislike of Rachel and flashed Brynna a frown. Sam wouldn't let herself be bought out with flattery. Just because she wasn't as selfish as Rachel didn't mean she wanted the HARP program here.

Why should she share her family, horses, or Jake

with strangers? And she didn't want sly kids spying on her friendship with the Phantom.

Just thinking of the silver stallion made Sam's pulse race. He needed her help. She had to protect him from wild horse rustlers who'd kill him for dog food. She didn't have time to be a good influence on Mikki.

*Get a grip*, Sam told herself. She was overreacting. Dad would never go for this idea. A proud, hard-working man who spoke only when he had to, Dad was the next thing to a hermit. He wanted nothing to do with the federal government and its programs.

Sam was about to tell Brynna to save her breath, when Dad nodded.

"Ms. Olson," Dad said, "you've got yourself a deal."

## Chapter Four ∾

VOICES SWIRLED around Sam, discussing and planning, but she just stood there, stunned.

"River Bend Ranch will help you out. We'll see how the pilot program goes," Dad cautioned. "No promises after that."

"Absolutely." Brynna nodded.

"We'd only have Mikki, to begin with, is that right?" Gram asked. "For an hour or two after school?"

"Right," Brynna said.

"I'd like to cook for that poor little thing . . ."

*Poor little thing?* Hadn't Gram heard the part about shoplifting and fighting?

". . . get some wholesome food into her." Gram clucked her tongue. "I suppose she'll go back to the foster home for meals, but I make nutritious after-school snacks. And then, if we get the program permanently . . ."

Sam's hands fisted so tightly, her fingernails bit

into her palms. The longer she let these plans roll ahead, the harder it would be to stop them.

Sam glanced toward the white truck. Mikki still sat inside, where she couldn't hear a thing.

"Besides Rachel, Jennifer Kenworthy's over at the Gold Dust Ranch. She's the foreman's daughter," Sam explained to Brynna. "And she's as good an influence as I am. Maybe better."

Sam knew her desperate tone had given her away when both Gram and Dad looked disappointed.

Brynna, on the other hand, seemed interested.

"If the work with Mikki turns out well, Jen could help next summer," Brynna said. "There's good funding for this program, enough to remodel the bunkhouse so you could host a whole group of girls. The program would pay for saddles, feed, and wages. You and Jen could be instructors."

Brynna stopped when Dad held out his hand in a move that clearly said *Halt*. But why was he smiling?

"When do we start?" Dad asked.

"I'll have Popcorn trailered out on Monday." Brynna looked as if she were making calculations. "If we start Mikki with him on Tuesday, that would give the horse time to settle in."

"Popcorn?" Gram asked.

Brynna's lips firmed into a straight line before she answered. "He's an albino gelding who's been 'shown who's boss' a few times too many. He's awfully shy, but he'll be a great match for Mikki."

Sam didn't see the logic in the woman's remark, but she kept quiet. She'd have time to work on Dad after Brynna left.

"Tuesday, then," Dad said, and stuck out his hand.

"Tuesday." Brynna shook Dad's hand. "Thanks so much, Wyatt. I hope it works out for all of us."

Not only had Brynna's brisk tone softened, but as she walked away, Dad watched her go with a small smile.

Frustrated down to her fingernails, Sam tackled her chores. She fed the dog, fed the chickens, topped off the water troughs, checked the hens' nests for eggs, then stood staring at Ace, Sweetheart, and the frightened buckskin.

She hadn't had a chance to groom Ace when she'd first ridden in. Now, she wanted to do it. She'd made a habit of pouring her troubles into Ace's attentive ears while she curried dirt and sweat from his coat. But it would be cruel to disturb the horses now. And selfish.

Sam walked into the shady barn and hung her green sweatshirt back on its nail. Selfishness. That was the feeling boiling inside her. But wasn't she allowed to be just a little stingy, when she'd just gotten her family back?

Sam sat on a hay bale. She tried not to look at the little buckskin. The mare was watching, waiting for Sam to do something scary.

Sam stared outside. The barn pasture was empty

of animals because several fence rails were down and a few were broken. The pasture reminded her of one of her worst mistakes since she'd come home and tried to fit back into ranch life.

Sam hadn't noticed the missing rails a month ago, when she'd left Buddy in that pen. While Sam was gone, the orphan calf had wandered away. Now Dad was pacing along the fence line.

He was getting ready to fix it. Not for her, but for Brynna.

Accidentally, Sam glanced at the buckskin. The mare's ears flattened against her neck and her nostrils flared.

Sam pretended to ignore the horse. She leaned back and stared into the barn's dark rafters. Overhead, a pigeon moved in its straw nest, trying to get comfy.

Sam knew how the bird felt. She was still adapting to ranch life. Gram and Dad tried to help, but each time she got used to them treating her like a child, they expected her to act like an adult.

Now Gram wanted to cook special meals for a stranger and fuss over *her*. Sam knew she sounded like a pouty little kid.

Her mind understood that Gram and Dad meant to do something good and charitable, but Sam's heart wanted to know why.

Why, why, *why* should they help this smart-mouthed kid named Mikki?

Lost in her own thoughts, Sam stopped watching Dad until he was just a few yards away. Sam shot to her feet, looking for something to do, but she didn't think fast enough.

The buckskin sucked in deep breaths, testing the air for threats.

Dad stood silhouetted against the outside brightness.

"Gram wants us to come eat some sandwiches and potato salad."

"Okay," Sam said. Her stomach growled and she felt lightheaded from eating nothing since last night's supper.

She knew she should politely follow her father inside and wait for her sulky mood to pass. But she didn't.

"Dad, we don't need more work around here. Especially with me at school all day."

"Outside work will lighten up as winter comes on. The girl will only be here five or six hours a week. I can spare Jake that much."

*Jake?* Sam muffled her screech of outrage, but it echoed in her mind.

Brynna had mentioned that Sam and Jen might be teaching the girls to ride. She'd said nothing about Jake. It must be Dad's idea, and that troubled Sam.

Sam tried to squash her jealousy. After all, Jake had taught *her* the patient Indian ways of working with horses. She couldn't imagine a better technique for soothing the hurts of horses and humans. Still . . .

"Jake, huh? I guess you don't agree with Brynna that I could handle it?"

Dad said nothing. His silence hurt.

"Just when I think you have faith in me, you expect me to fail."

"I didn't expect it." Dad spoke slowly. "You surprised me, sayin' BLM should send a ruined mustang and that child over to Slocum's."

"But when BLM offered you the job tracking wild horses, you didn't do it." Sam didn't add, *and we could have used the money.* "Why did you say yes this time?"

Dad nodded toward the buckskin mare, and even that faint movement sent her sidling away from the fence. But Dad didn't answer Sam's question. He asked one, instead.

"Why didn't you leave that mare up at Lost Canyon?"

Sam's spirits fell. She'd been so sure Dad would understand.

"She was—they had her blindfolded. She was standing in the dark, alone. I couldn't leave her there."

"Neither could I," Dad said.

"But, Dad—"

"That's my answer, Samantha. Chew on it."

Later that evening, Jen called to explain why she'd missed their early-morning ride.

Her cold had gotten worse.

"I didn't oversleep," Jen said, sniffing. "I was up getting dressed, but my mom heard me coughing and wouldn't let me go."

It took Sam a second to understand, but if she took the word that sounded like *bomb* and substituted *mom*, Jen's sentence made sense.

"That's what I figured," Sam said. "But I've got so much to tell you. And part of it involves the Phantom."

Jen gasped. "Talk fast. Mom only gave me ten minutes. Then, I have to go back to bed."

"Okay, but—oops." Sam lost her grip on the phone. She was juggling the receiver as she folded laundry. "Sorry I dropped you. I think Gram and Dad are giving me time to figure out how lucky I am," Sam told Jen.

"Lucky?"

"Lucky that I have a decent home and people who care enough about me to make me fold a mountain of laundry taller than I am," Sam said.

When Jen made a confused sound, Sam asked, "Have you heard of the HARP program?"

"Sure. They pair juvenile delinquents with problem horses, then step back and watch to see who kills who first."

"Jen, you're terrible." Sam shook her head at her friend's sarcasm.

Jen's laughter provoked more coughing. When

she finally stopped, she asked, "That's the program, though, right? They have it in California and New Mexico."

"Sort of," Sam said. "Except Brynna Olson and Dad have worked it out so that the Nevada program's first kid—"

"Just *one* delinquent in all of Nevada? I'm not buying that."

"—will meet the horse here. Then Jake and I will work with the kid and the horse. The mustang is an albino named Popcorn."

When Jen made a throat-clearing sound that sounded like envy, Sam told her Brynna's plan.

"It's a government program and there's enough money set aside that if things work out with Popcorn and Mikki—that's the first girl's name—they might send more kids during the summer, and Brynna said they might need you as an instructor, too."

"Wow." Jen sighed. "How cool is that?"

Would Jen like the idea so much if she were sharing her own parents?

"But wait," Jen said. "Do you really believe my mom, who home-schooled me because she didn't want me corrupted by outside influences, is going to—"

Jen's voice faded as her hand muffled the telephone mouthpiece. "Yes, Mom, I know it's been . . . But I feel much—" Suddenly, Jen's voice was clear. "Sam, I have to get off now."

Disappointed that the conversation had ended so

soon, Sam teased her friend.

"Oh, that's fine. I didn't really want to tell you about the wild horse rustlers."

"What?" Jen's squeak triggered her coughs all over again.

"And how the Phantom came to the rescue—" Sam stopped taunting Jen and bit her lip. She probably shouldn't mention the beautiful buckskin, either.

"Don't forget *anything*," Jen whispered. "I want details."

That night, Gram served up a lecture along with dinner.

"As soon as Brynna mentioned this program, I started reading up on it," Gram said.

*And how long ago was that?* Sam wondered. Gram had seemed surprised, but apparently only Sam had been kept out of the loop.

"There's not a lot of data so far, but it's working. In most other programs, seven out of ten kids are back in trouble inside of a year. With HARP, it's three out of ten."

"If they get back in trouble," Sam mused, "can they come back to work with the mustangs?"

"Whatever do you mean?"

"I was just thinking," Sam said, remembering the joy on Mikki's face as she watched the horses gallop across their pasture. "If I were a bad kid, I might mess up again so that I could come back and work with the horses."

"Samantha Anne, I don't know why I try to treat you like an adult, when all you want to do is joke." Gram whacked the wooden tongs back into the salad bowl.

She *hadn't* been joking. Sam looked to her father for help. He balanced the lettuce on his fork for a minute, studying her.

"I think she's serious," he said.

"I am."

"Well, all right," Gram said. "Sometimes it's hard to tell."

"You know what else I was wondering?" Sam asked. "Why we couldn't use that buckskin mare instead of the albino Brynna was talking about." Sam looked from Gram to Dad.

Sam tried to imagine Mikki giving the buckskin the gentle handling she needed. She couldn't.

No, when she stared at the kitchen wall, imagining it was a movie screen, the girl she saw loving that frightened horse was herself.

## Chapter Five ∾

$S$AM DREAMED of the Phantom. In her dream, a giant swan floated down the river, gradually changing into the curve-necked, broad-chested stallion. But he didn't lose his wings. The mighty stallion launched into flight, and Sam woke to the rustling of feathers.

As she dressed in boots and jeans, Sam couldn't shake the feeling that the Phantom had actually been near. She'd fallen asleep yearning to see him, wishing she could go to the river, even though she'd known he wouldn't come to her.

The Phantom was the leader, the protector of his herd. After yesterday's near disaster, she knew he wouldn't leave the horses alone, even in their isolated valley in the Calico Mountains.

She couldn't read the stallion's mind, but Jake had tutored her in horse psychology. The Phantom wouldn't lead his band back up the narrow trail to Lost Canyon, even though the water seeping from the rock walls was sweet. The narrow trail, funneling into that tight trap, would have frightened the horses, so the Phantom would take the mares to an open area.

They'd be more visible, but that drawback worked to the animals' advantage. They'd see anything that could see them and have plenty of time to use their best weapon: speed.

War Drum Flats. That's where they'd go. The pond was scooped from the level sagebrush— and piñon pine–dotted land that lay at the foot of the trail up to Lost Canyon. Best of all, a ridge overlooked the area, so the Phantom could keep watch and use his trumpeting neigh to warn his family of danger.

*Dusk*, Sam thought. She'd do all of her chores and homework and ride Ace to War Drum Flats just as the sun went down.

Sam avoided the mirror and finger-combed her hair as she trotted downstairs.

The kitchen was already warm and filled with the smell of frying ham and eggs.

Sam kissed Gram and kept moving toward the door.

"Biscuits will be done in about five minutes," Gram said.

"I just want to check on the buckskin," Sam announced.

"Go on, then," Gram said, "But hurry back."

She had to make sure the buckskin hadn't escaped. Though the corral was too small to allow the running start needed to leap the fence, wings still fluttered in Sam's imagination.

Sam started to open the door, then let it close without leaving the kitchen.

"What's Brynna Olson doing here?" Sam asked.

Gram turned from the stove and stood just behind Sam, looking over her shoulder through the window.

"My, my, I don't know. I wonder if she knows Wyatt's already ridden out?" Gram pushed her glasses farther up her nose, but the white truck parked in the ranch yard was still there. "Well, dear, run on out and ask her in for breakfast."

Sam might have protested if she hadn't disappointed Gram yesterday. It would be a waste of time, anyway. Gram always got her way, sooner or later.

Ace's nicker floated to Sam, but Brynna didn't turn to look at her. She watched the barn corral and stayed still to keep from startling the buckskin. The golden brown mare shifted nervously, but she stood facing the barn.

Sam sighed. It was sad that the little mustang was happier staring into the darkness.

"Gram says—"

"I didn't come for breakfast, Sam. I came to talk with you." Brynna didn't look away from the horses, but Sam stood beside her now, and she saw the dark circles under the redhead's eyes. Brynna's tone made Sam fear she was to blame for the woman's sleepless night.

Brynna wasn't wearing her uniform today. She wore gray cords and a teal pullover. Far from making her red hair and blue eyes more vivid, the teal emphasized the fact that Brynna's eyes looked faded and tired.

"I haven't been able to track down her owner yet," Brynna said. "But she was adopted by Mrs. Rose Bloom of Caspar, Wyoming, who did enter a name for the mare." Brynna paused for effect. "Dark Sunshine."

"It's perfect," Sam said. "Not just her color, but— everything."

"That may be all the woman did right," Brynna said. "Mrs. Bloom's phone is disconnected. There's nothing in BLM records saying she *didn't* gain title to her last May." Brynna sighed. "Which means, she might have sold the horse legally since then."

Brynna raised one eyebrow as she regarded Sam.

"So, one of those rustlers could own her?" Sam asked. "Maybe I really did steal her." Sam thought of the mare, thirsty and bewildered in that mountain trap. "But I'm not sorry."

"There are laws against mistreating animals, and they broke them. If they filed a complaint against you, I doubt a judge would take it seriously."

Sam felt a flush of warmth at Brynna's support, until the woman went on in her cold, official voice.

"The brand inspector at the auction yards in Mineral says no horses came in with fresh brands."

Anyone would have spotted a fresh brand. Sam remembered Buddy's. For days after her pet calf had been branded, Sam thought the mark looked exactly like what it was—a second-degree burn.

"That's good, I guess," Sam said. "But you'd have to be really dumb to brand a wild horse and try to sell him the same day, wouldn't you?"

"Yes," Brynna said. "But I think the criminal genius is a myth."

Sam laughed. If the three rustlers she'd seen were representative of crooks . . . well, only one of the three had seemed very smart.

"The brand inspector saw animals without brands," Brynna said, "but none appeared to be range horses. There were only three—two packhorses from Elko and a very old Shetland pony."

At that, Sam couldn't repress a frown.

Neither could Brynna, though she worked at being tough. Sam didn't know if she worked so hard at it because she had a responsible job, or because she was a woman in a mostly male profession, or because she was hiding a soft heart.

If Brynna hadn't hated the thought of people selling horses for pet food once they outlived their usefulness, she wouldn't have mentioned the Shetland pony.

*Maybe I'm not in trouble after all*, Sam thought. *Maybe thoughts of pitiful horses kept Brynna awake last night.* Suddenly, though, Brynna changed the subject.

"Mikki Small has had three stepfathers in the last four years. She's lived in eight different apartments and gone to seven schools between fourth grade and sixth grade."

Sam flinched at Brynna's accusing tone.

"That would be really hard," Sam said. She didn't say anything to fill the silence swelling between them. Instead, she touched a splinter on the fence. She'd have to get some sandpaper and smooth it down before a horse got hurt.

"I don't know why it happened, but Mikki was telling the truth when she said her mother sent her away."

Sam kept trying to smooth the splinter down as she remembered how she'd felt the few times Dad had given Brynna extra-long looks. She'd hated it. Even though her reaction made no sense, she felt like he was choosing Brynna over her. The feeling cut like a knife, then kept aching each time she thought of it.

How much worse must it be for Mikki, whose mom had married three different guys and then sent her away? And Mikki was only twelve.

All at once, Sam realized her hand had reached up to touch her breastbone. She didn't want to sympathize with Mikki, but her heart didn't know that. Deliberately, she put her hand back on the fence.

"Couldn't you get in trouble for telling me this?"

"Sure," Brynna said. "I could probably get fired."

Sam took a deep breath and glanced back toward

the house. Gram would be waiting.

"But, how about the way she refused to shake Gram's hand? And the way she squared off with Jake? And . . ." Sam hesitated as a blush crawled up her cheeks. "I know it's no big deal, but she looks at me like I'm a . . . a hick."

"I'll tell you what you look like to her, Samantha. You look like the luckiest girl in the world. You have people who love you, and horses, and a future."

Sam didn't cry, but when Ace ambled to the fence and whuffled his soft lips over her fingers, she came close.

She didn't admit she felt like a spoiled brat. She didn't tell Brynna she'd make a great psychologist, either. But both were true.

After she'd finished her homework, Sam worked with Dallas. One reason the River Bend foreman was well liked was his willingness to work. Although the gray-haired buckaroo let it be known his only talent was work done from horseback, he'd dirty his hands with most any chore.

The chore of the day was repairing the chicken coop.

For weeks, Gram had suspected her Rhode Island Red hens were laying more eggs than she was getting. Something, she insisted, was slipping into the coop at night and stealing eggs.

By the time the hailstorm came and the hens

resumed laying, Gram had also noticed the coop could use tightening up. Sam was awarded the job, but Dallas had offered to help.

Now, he grunted as he settled his saddle-weary bones into a squat next to the coop.

"Snakes, weasels, ground squirrels could all get through something that size," Dallas said as he examined an opening in the wire. He measured it with his middle and index fingers. "There's no room for a raccoon, though they do like eggs."

Sam liked working with Dallas. As long as she did her share, he never criticized. And maybe because he'd known her since she was a toddler, Dallas never thought her questions were dumb.

"Would any of those animals hurt the chickens?" Sam asked.

"Probably not," Dallas said. "If a critter ate one of these big fluffies"—he gestured at the fat hens, whose feathers puffed up at the disturbance caused by the two humans—"it likely couldn't get out again. Plus, they'd set up a ruckus that would wake us, or Blaze.

"Come spring, though, if we have any chicks, they'll gobble them down for sure."

Sam felt a little queasy, thinking of a chick-size lump in the gliding length of a snake. She didn't say anything, but Dallas must have noticed her expression.

"What we need to do is take off this old chicken wire." Dallas gestured to the screening within the wooden frame of the enclosure. "Then we'll replace it with new. After that, we'll put out the word we need a rooster. A mean one. Anything comes sneaking along after that is in trouble. All it needs to do is stick its head in, and the rooster will grab on and flog it till you can fold it up like your Gram's hanky."

Sam worked quickly, lulled by the low clucking of the hens.

The chickens were set free daily to peck at table scraps and bugs. Dark Sunshine acted as if she'd never seen such creatures. The buckskin slung her head over the top rail of the fence. Ears pricked forward, eyes tracking every movement, she watched the hens, trembling with fascination.

"Look." Sam nudged Dallas and nodded toward the mare.

"She's showing you that she can be smart and interested," Dallas said. "Now, you just got to figure how to get her to look at you like she does those chickens."

"I wish I could." Sam sighed. "I'm worried about BLM returning her to her owner."

"Oh, I think she'll be sticking around River Bend for a good long time," Dallas said.

"I hope so. Whoever owns her doesn't deserve her," Sam grumbled. "I'd buy her from them if Dad hadn't forced me to put my reward money in savings."

Just a few weeks ago, Linc Slocum had offered a

huge reward for the return of his Appaloosa mare, Apache Hotspot. Using horse sense and her talent with a camera, Sam earned the reward by unmasking the renegade stallion who'd stolen mares right out of their home pastures.

But Dad didn't believe in shopping sprees. He'd allowed her to buy a camera of her own, small gifts for him and Gram, a soft leather headstall for Jake's upcoming birthday, and a new well pump.

She'd had to fight him on that purchase. Sam and Dad had stood toe-to-toe, each with arms crossed. Sam figured Dad finally realized she was every bit as stubborn as he was and the time they were wasting made him give in.

If every other penny hadn't gone into her college savings account, Sam knew she could have convinced Dark Sunshine's owners to sell her.

An afternoon breeze blew over the sagebrush by the time Sam rode out on Ace. She'd had to display all her finished homework and promise to return in time for dinner, but at last she was riding.

Ace moved at a rocking chair lope across the high desert, and Sam thought maybe Brynna had been right. With the wind in her face, a spirited horse carrying her across starkly beautiful land and love waiting for her at home, she felt awfully lucky.

They'd almost reached War Drum Flats when Sam leaned forward to pat Ace's neck and saw the horse.

At first, peering through the frame of Ace's ears, Sam took the palomino for a lone mustang.

The mustang had wings.

Sam thought of her weird dream, then shook her head. Impossible. But something *was* flapping out from the horse's body.

Ace's stride didn't change, but Sam felt him grow tense beneath her. "What is it, boy?"

Sam squinted. She wished for a camera to bring the scene into focus. Then, all at once, she recognized the movement.

Stirrup leathers bounced out with each galloping step the palomino took, but the saddle above them was empty.

Sam urged Ace into a run, planning a path that would intersect with the palomino's. Out on the range, with darkness coming on, a riderless horse could only mean trouble.

## Chapter Six ๑

THE PALOMINO WAS ready to stop running. He slowed to a trot, a walk, and finally fell into step beside Ace, so that Sam could snag his reins.

Even if Sam hadn't recognized the palomino, she might have guessed his owner by the horse's trappings. The silver conchos glittering on his noseband matched those decorating his black leather saddle. It was parade gear, and the only man in northern Nevada who'd tack up his horse this way for a Sunday afternoon ride was Linc Slocum.

"What are you doing, horse, running away from home?"

She wouldn't blame him. Champ belonged to Slocum, and the man compensated for his mediocre riding skill by using harsh bits and spurs. The palomino wasn't bleeding from spur gouges today, but his dark lips were smeared with foam.

Sam scanned the range. Slocum was nowhere in

sight, and she was glad. For the first time, she'd have a chance to help this horse.

Crooning to keep the palomino calm, Sam dismounted and ground-tied Ace.

Today, Slocum rode with a spade bit. From outside, it was a thing of beauty, silver mounted with fine engraving, but inside a horse's mouth, it could be a torture device. The three-inch metal spade worked on the tenderest parts of the horse's mouth.

According to Dallas, the bit worked elegantly in the hands of an expert rider. But Slocum was no expert. Dallas said giving Slocum reins connected to a spade bit and expecting him to ride well was like giving a monkey a straight razor and expecting him to give you a nice, close shave.

She'd have to return Champ to Slocum, but she had time to adjust the bridle so that the bit moved with less severity.

Sam had just finished and remounted when Slocum appeared on the horizon, limping toward her in high-heeled cowboy boots.

She held Ace's reins in her left hand, Champ's in her right, and the palomino followed along nicely.

"You're a good horse, Champ," Sam said to the horse, "but it's just like your boss to get himself stranded when I'm in a hurry."

The good news was that she was nearly to War Drum Flats and Slocum's Gold Dust Ranch was only a couple of miles away. Once she got Slocum back in the saddle, she should have the area to herself. She just hoped he hadn't created such a commotion that he'd frightened off all the wildlife in the area from horses to jackrabbits.

"Well now," Slocum bawled when he got within range, "aren't you a sight for sore eyes!"

Sam might have said the same, but she would've dropped the last three words. Slocum's plaid shirt and jeans weren't extraordinary, but Sam couldn't stop staring at his boots.

Working cowboys wore their jeans over their boot tops, but Slocum tucked his in to show off the red and yellow cutouts and fancy green stitching. The boots matched the silver-mounted tack for flashiness.

Though he had to have been walking for some time, balancing his barrel-shaped body atop his slant-heeled boots, Linc Slocum looked in good spirits. His slicked-back black hair lay in place and his white grin in his flushed face made him look like an advertisement for quick-tanning lotion.

"Hello," Sam greeted him. "Going someplace special?"

Slocum didn't realize she was referring to his gaudy attire.

"Just to get my horse," he puffed, taking the reins from her hand. "Champ decided to give me an opportunity to see if the moon really is made of green cheese."

Sam managed a small laugh. Slocum loved using

expressions he thought were Western. If they'd come out of Dallas's mouth, they might have worked, but somehow Slocum didn't get the timing right.

"But seriously," Slocum amended, "what's goin' on over at your place these days?"

"Just the usual," Sam said.

Slocum loved gossip, but he rarely got stories even approximately straight. Sam couldn't mention the HARP program, wild horse rustlers, or the buckskin mare she'd sort of stolen unless she wanted to hear a twisted version of each item as she climbed onto the school bus tomorrow morning.

"Well, I've got some good news."

Sam braced. Slocum's "good news" almost never was.

"I'm going to start breeding Brahma bulls t'sell to rodeo contractors. Now, ain't that fine?"

Sam could force her lips to smile, but she couldn't erase the pictures of disaster playing in her mind. A man who'd accidentally hired a criminal to help him capture the Phantom, who gave his daughter thousands of dollars for clothes, makeup, and anything else she wanted, who couldn't stay on his own horse or dress for the rough country he lived in, should not get near two-ton animals bred for their vile tempers. She might be only thirteen, but even she knew better.

Slocum didn't wait for her opinion. "Ought to have them delivered and in their new pens about two weeks from now. I wanted to invite Wyatt and

Grace—and you, of course—to a special little Brahma-que."

"You're going to eat them?"

"No, 'course not, honey. That's just a little play on words. I'll have my staff grill up lobster tails and T-bone steaks. Think you all would like to come?"

"Sure."

Sam knew Dad mourned the loss of every minute spent in Slocum's company, but he'd want to see the cattle. And Gram embraced any excuse for a party. She'd come carrying a chocolate layer cake or lemon meringue pie that would draw more compliments than Slocum's gourmet fare.

"Well, you saved me a trip," Slocum said. "And if you would, tell Jake Ely's dad—what's his name? Luke?—that they're invited, too."

Sam would have enjoyed seeing Slocum at Three Ponies Ranch. Jake's parents might have maintained straight faces at Slocum's getup, but Jake and his six older brothers would've had a good laugh.

Slocum sawed at his reins. Though trying to signal the palomino to wheel into a turn, Slocum only succeeded in pulling the animal's head from side to side. With role models like Linc Slocum at the Gold Dust Ranch, maybe it was better Brynna had chosen the River Bend to host HARP.

Champ obeyed the reins, rolling his eyes and tossing his head. Sam thought the gelding's moves were done from habit rather than pain, and she was glad she'd made the adjustments. Slocum would never notice. Already, he was kicking the palomino into a run.

"*Adios, muchacho!*" Slocum yelled, then headed for home.

Sam waved.

*Muchacho.* Slocum's Spanish was even worse than his English. He'd called her a little boy. On the other hand, Sam didn't mind what he called her, as long as he left her alone to wait for the Phantom.

Five more minutes. Sam considered her watch, knowing she shouldn't wait longer for her horse to appear. In only twenty-five minutes, she was supposed to be home. It would take her that long to ride to the River Bend bridge. Then she still had to cool Ace, strip off his tack, and brush him before releasing him into the corral. And who knew how long that would take if Dark Sunshine tried to escape?

It started to rain. Drops pattered on the brim of Sam's old brown Stetson. She couldn't sit there any longer, waiting for the wild one who wouldn't come.

She missed him so much, her eyes were fooled by a curtain of rain wafting down the hill. For a minute, she thought it was the silver stallion.

"C'mon, Ace. We're just going to get soaked if we stay." Sam lay the reins against the gelding's neck, but he didn't move. "Ace?"

Sam turned back and looked again. Pale and

silent as a wisp of cloud, the Phantom led his herd down the cleft in the hillside, toward water.

He was so perfect, she didn't even feel disloyal to Ace. Ace was her friend. The Phantom was perfection, a king among horses. Tonight he moved with a deerlike caution she'd never seen before. With swift, head-swiveling movements, he tasted the wind and rain. He studied every bobbing bush to see if it hid a man. He sampled each scent for the stench of a human.

The Phantom paused, one foreleg lifted in midstride, when he noticed Sam. She saw his nostrils distend, saw a shudder run through him as he decided she could be trusted.

Behind him, the mares moved in an uneasy swirl. Then he came on, bolder and faster than before. With hammering hooves, he bolted into the water hole. The stallion dipped up a quick sip. He answered the mares' questioning nickers with a shake of his head. For a second, his eyes were veiled with white mane. And then he cleared the way, racing toward the windswept ridge that was his lookout post.

Sam watched him go. Each of the mustangs in the water hole was beautiful. The tiger dun, the blood bay mares who must be twins, the sorrel foal who'd nearly been lost to the herd just yesterday, but Sam spared them only a glance.

The silver stallion, tail streaming like a waterfall as he navigated the path, was what she'd come for.

The stallion knew her.

Horses didn't forget, so he must remember her mistakes, and she didn't pretend to be nice, or polite or braver than she was, around horses. This one, least of all. And yet he trusted her.

Before he reached the hill crest, the Phantom stopped. He pirouetted in a space that looked too narrow for his muscled quarters, and looked down, watching.

The tiger dun leaped from knee-deep water to the shore and the others followed, but Sam couldn't see a thing. What had frightened them? Were they over-reacting to buck brush crackling under the big rain-drops that continued to fall?

The stallion forced his way against the tide of flee-ing mares, but they kept on, and Sam realized Ace was jittering beneath her, grunting a troubled sound as his head angled toward the highway.

Sam heard the hiss of tires on wet pavement.

Ace had heard passing traffic hundreds of times, though, and so had the mustangs. And any vehicle would have to pull off the highway and navigate a bumpy dirt road to reach them.

The wild horses would have plenty of time to run.

But this wasn't just any vehicle. A mud-yellow truck had left the highway. Its pinging engine labored and its tires spun as it roared onto the dirt road.

And then Sam knew why the Phantom had turned. Once more, he was protecting her, herding her with his mares to safety.

Before the stallion reached them, Sam clapped her heels to Ace's sides.

"Go!" Sam leaned low on the gelding's neck and called to his backcast ears.

In a flurry of churning hooves, the Phantom and Ace sideswiped each other, pinning Sam's leg between them. She gasped, but kept Ace aimed after the wild mares. The tiger dun was leading the herd to safety, and Sam wanted to follow.

By now the rustlers must know someone had rescued Dark Sunshine. They knew someone was onto their crime, and though there was little chance they knew it was her, Sam wasn't going to stick around to make sure.

Her Stetson blew off her head and only the stampede string kept it from flying away. The braided horsehair string sawed against Sam's throat, and she blinked against the rain pelting her face. But running with the mustangs was glorious, uncontrolled. She grabbed handfuls of mane and clung low on Ace's neck, filling her lungs with the smell of wet rocks and hot horsehide.

The horses jostled, pressing tight together into a dark gorge thick with brush. Stickers ripped Sam's jeans, scratched her hands. A dark horse built like a rhino jammed past, and Ace staggered.

Then the mustangs stopped. Their breath hung in the moist air. Sam hadn't been running, but her heart beat as if she had. Surrounded by the herd, she was the only one making a sound. She tried to muffle her panting.

The Phantom stood nose-to-nose with Ace. Through strands of silvery forelock, he watched Sam. His head bobbed silently, as if in greeting, and their eyes held.

The pinging of the truck engine echoed as it continued up the mountain, then braked to a stop.

Were the rustlers looking for horses or for her? It didn't matter. If the men found the mustangs, they'd find her. Sam stared into the Phantom's dark eyes. This moment, she was one of the herd, in safety or in danger.

A tremor ran through the herd as a truck door slammed and footsteps crunched on dirt. Sam closed her eyes, wishing the darkness behind her own lids could cover her.

On her first day back in Nevada, she and Dad had seen a helicopter herding mustangs toward a trap. In a blink, they'd scattered over the range, then vanished.

"Mustangs have secret getaway trails," Dad had told her, trails humans couldn't find. That's where she was, hiding like a prey animal, waiting for predators to lose patience and leave.

Finally, they did. The truck's door slammed and its engine started. The sound of spinning tires and spattering mud grew fainter and fainter.

The Phantom backed out of the thicket. The mares followed, and Sam kept Ace reined in, making him wait for last.

As they emerged, Sam discovered the rain had stopped, but dusk had turned into darkness.

She glanced at her watch. The blue-green numbers glowed. She was a full half hour late for dinner right now, and she still had to ride home.

The lead mare clattered up the hillside with her family close behind. A pale shadow against the darkness, the Phantom followed after.

*Good-bye, Zanzibar.* Sam sent the message with her mind. Though she was probably the only human on this rain-slick hillside, she didn't call the stallion by his secret name.

Sam tried to look away, then she was glad she couldn't. Halfway up the windswept ridge, he paused and looked back.

Once he went on, Sam started toward home. This time, it wasn't her fault she was late. Gram and Dad would be worried, and she'd tell them the truth. All of it.

She'd felt scared hiding with the herd. Those rustlers were more trouble than she could handle on her own.

## Chapter Seven ৩১

THE RANCH YARD was flooded with light. Brightness glowed from inside the barn and the kitchen door stood open. The headlights from the Elys' idling truck lit the path from the River Bend bridge to the two-story white house, which looked more welcoming than ever before.

Jake was there. Who else had Gram and Dad called?

From the bridge, Sam saw Dad, Gram, and Dallas talking on the front porch. Blaze barked at her approach, and they all looked up. Dallas gave a salute from the brim of his hat to Dad, then walked across the yard toward the bunkhouse.

"You okay?" Dallas asked as he passed through the beams of Jake's headlights. When Sam nodded, he added, "Horse okay?"

"He's fine. He's a great horse. We just ran into some trouble." Sam tried to keep her voice from shaking.

"Let me take him," Dallas said, moving to Ace's head. "You'd best tell the rest of it to the boss. Pronto. He hasn't called out the *whole* county yet, but he needs to know."

Sam had managed to keep her voice steady, but now, as Dallas led Ace away, her knees felt watery and weak.

Jake still sat inside the truck. She couldn't see his expression, but Sam knew he'd be mad. More like furious. He hated worrying about her, but whenever she told him to stop, he always went ballistic.

Gram had gone back into the kitchen, probably to get on the phone and call off the search. Arms folded, Dad leaned against a porch post, waiting.

This was a Western thing. Ranch life demanded she be self-sufficient and not cause trouble for anyone else.

*All I have to do is walk across the yard and explain.* Sam took a few steps, though she wanted to sit down right there in the dirt, pull her knees up, let her forehead rest on them and wait for Dad to come to her. But Sam kept walking. Blaze licked her hand, whining as he bounced along beside her.

"You caught Slocum's horse for him, but that was more than an hour ago," Dad said.

"Yeah," Sam answered. If Slocum knew she'd been missing, Rachel would know. The drama would be all over school by the end of first period, but it didn't matter. She'd almost made it to the porch.

"You look a little pale." Dad uncrossed his arms as he studied her. "How 'bout sittin' down to tell me what went wrong."

Sam lowered herself to the top step and pulled her coat close against the wet wind.

Dad leaned down to rest a hand on her shoulder. "Want to go inside?"

Sam shook her head no.

"The rustlers came back. I don't know if they were looking for horses or for me —" Sam heard Dad suck in a breath as if he'd been punched in the stomach. "But I had to hide until they went away."

"It's all right, honey." Dad settled on the step beside her. Sam leaned into the circle of his arm and began to tell him everything.

It turned out Rachel Slocum didn't find Sam's adventure worth talking about at school. For that, Sam was grateful.

Jake knew, of course, and Dad had insisted Sam describe the truck to Brynna, and Sam had told Jen.

Only one thing changed after that night of hiding. Sam wasn't allowed to go anywhere alone.

That was why, on Tuesday afternoon, Sam stood talking with Jen instead of starting the mile-long walk home.

"You don't have to wait with me," Sam told Jen. "Gram will be picking me up any minute."

"And miss all the excitement when the bad guys

come?" Jen twirled the tail of one skinny white-blond braid and peered over the top of her dark-framed glasses. "Oh, no. I missed part one of this adventure. No way are you going to leave me out of part two." Jen was almost over her cold, and her sharp sense of humor was back.

"I don't think there'll be a part two," Sam said. "Rangers are looking for the rustlers so they'd be dumb to come back here. Besides, they just want Dark Sunshine, not me."

"So you're really not scared?" Jen asked.

Sam stood quiet for a minute, taking inventory of how she felt. The terror she'd felt hiding with the horses had faded.

"Not really," Sam said, and it was the truth, until Jen's emphatic nod.

"Good."

"Why 'good'?" Sam asked.

"Thursday we have a half day because of teacher meetings, right?" Jen reminded her. "So, unless you're a lousy friend who doesn't care anything about my feelings or the expert tutoring I'm giving you in math . . ."

"Take a breath, then get to the point," Sam said.

". . . you'll take me up to the rustlers' trap."

Sam didn't ask why. Jen's curiosity mirrored her own, and Sam knew that if the situation had been reversed, she would want to ride up and see the site of all the excitement.

Sam had no reason not to go, but she offered a deterrent. "The federal rangers have already been up there, you know."

Jen rubbed her hands together in anticipation. "Suppose they left yellow crime scene tape, or some of that magic dust they use to lift fingerprints?"

"I don't know if they do that. Besides, you want to be a vet, not a cop."

"I'm keeping my options open," Jen said. "So you'll do it?"

"I'll do it, but . . ." Sam lowered her voice as if she might be overheard. "If they'll let me, I want to start gentling Dark Sunshine."

"I hope you keep her," Jen said. "Then Silly won't be the only neurotic horse in the neighborhood."

Jen joked about Silk Stockings, her high-strung palomino, but she loved her as much as Sam loved Ace. Jen had come over after school yesterday to see Popcorn and Dark Sunshine, and she and Sam had been analyzing the mustangs' behavior ever since.

"You've got a lot to undo with the mare, and she's going to be unpredictable for a long time. Miss Olson's smart to use Popcorn with the HARP program. He looks like he has some draft blood."

"So he should be calmer," Sam agreed, "once he lets us get near him. And he doesn't have that haunted look."

*Unlike Dark Sunshine.* Sam didn't say the words, just pushed her bangs back and tried not to recall how the buckskin had wanted to follow the other horses into the trailer. She hadn't cared where they were going, she just hadn't wanted to be left behind.

"Besides," Sam said, "Popcorn wasn't abused on purpose. They told Brynna they tried to break him just like they'd seen in movies. The day after they got him, they snubbed him to a post, saddled him, and climbed on. He bucked. He ran through a fence. He was impossible to catch, so after a while they just ignored him."

"Hi, nice to meet you," Jen said, pretending to be Popcorn's owner. "I know you've lived free all your life, but let me tie your head at a weird angle, throw something heavy on your back, yank something tight around your middle, and oh, yeah, now I'm going to jump on you! What are people thinking?"

"You're going to be a good vet," Sam told her friend. "You think like a horse. But Brynna says Popcorn didn't hurt anyone, in spite of all that. In fact, BLM didn't take him away from the adopters — they returned him."

"Like shoes that didn't fit." Jen made a growling noise.

"Here comes Gram." Sam waved at the boatlike Buick coming toward them, but Jen wasn't finished grumbling.

"Some people don't understand horses have feelings," Jen said.

"I guess not." But all at once Sam thought not of

Dark Sunshine but of Mikki. Mikki's mother hadn't exactly returned her, but she *had* sent her away.

The seventh grade troublemaker would arrive today for her first session with Popcorn and Jake. She deserved a little sympathy, Sam thought, so she'd give it to her. After all, how hard could that be?

Mikki's hands perched on her hips. She wore tight jeans and a pink nylon top that bared her tummy. Someone should tell her it was too short, and that her blond hair was sticking out like wet feathers.

But Jake had already told the girl something, and she didn't like it one bit.

"You want me to sit in the dirt inside that pen, just *sit* there, for an *hour*?" she demanded of Jake. "I hope you're not getting paid for this."

Jake didn't wear chaps today. He wore clean jeans and a short-sleeved white shirt. He'd even removed his hat to talk with the girl. Now he pulled it on, covering the shiny black hair he tied back with a leather string.

"You're not, are you?" Mikki said, but Jake only walked into the round corral, leaving Mikki outside.

Mikki whirled on Sam. "Why isn't he saying anything?"

Mikki had just arrived, and already Sam was counting the minutes until the girl's counselor came back to collect her.

"Huh?" Mikki said. "What's his problem?"

"My guess is that he's treating you like he would a colt putting up a fuss. He's just waiting for you to finish, so he can go on with business."

"Like a horse?" Mikki asked.

"Yeah, and I'd say you're lucky. He almost never treats me that well. He really likes horses."

"Are you joking?"

"Not really," Sam admitted. "Jake and I grew up together, and he calls me Brat."

Mikki's lips twisted in a dubious expression. "So should I go in there?" She jerked her thumb toward the round pen.

"In a minute." Sam held up her finger. What she had to say next would be awkward, but if she kept quiet, the girl could get in big trouble. "My dad's pretty easygoing—"

"Yeah, they all start out that way," Mikki scoffed.

"Well, he's been like that for thirteen years I know of," Sam snapped. "Anyway, there's one thing he won't put up with: smoking around the barn."

"Why should I care? You don't see me smoking."

"No." Sam tried to keep her hands from closing into fists. "I don't see it, but you smell like cigarette smoke. If they don't care what you do at that place you're staying, fine, but the straw in our barn could go up like that." Sam snapped her fingers under the girl's nose. "If Dad catches you smoking, you'll be out of here so fast it'll make your head spin."

The sparkle in Mikki's eyes said she'd tried to

provoke Sam into losing control. And she'd won.

*Get a grip*, Sam told herself as she opened the gate to the round pen. Popcorn sidestepped, eyes rolling. Mikki wasn't the only one who was supposed to get something from HARP. She might not even be the most deserving one.

Popcorn was tall for a mustang, about fifteen hands, and he watched her with crystal-blue eyes. Built like a heavy Quarter horse, the gelding had already started growing a fuzzy winter coat that made Sam think of a stuffed toy. But when Sam leaned her head in to talk with Jake, who sat on the ground to her right, Popcorn backed away a few fearful steps, then banged his whole body against the fence as if to escape.

"You comin' in?" Jake asked.

"No." Sam heard Mikki behind her, so she leaned down and whispered to Jake, "I'll watch from outside and leave you in here with the wild things."

Jake grunted and motioned Mikki in. Sam stepped aside, but as Mikki passed, she shot Sam an angry look. She didn't like being left out.

Sam smiled as she withdrew from the corral and closed the gate. One of Jake's horse strategies built on the fact that they were herd animals.

Maybe the technique worked with kids, too.

Sam peered through the slats of the round pen and watched Jake, Mikki, and Popcorn. As usual, Jake didn't waste words.

"Sit there." He nodded to a place midway between Popcorn and himself. "Lean back. You're gonna be there a while."

"A whole hour?" Mikki didn't whine now that she was watching the mustang.

"How long ya got?" Jake asked. "He can't trust you if you're never around."

"Don't I know it," Mikki said, then plopped cross-legged in the dirt.

Sam glanced at her watch. She'd bet Mikki couldn't sit for five minutes without wiggling or talking.

Two minutes later, Mikki blurted, "What am I supposed to be doing?" Popcorn bolted at her voice, and Mikki made a soft sound of regret. "I'm not doing it right, but I don't know how. Tell me."

"Not much you can do wrong," Jake said. "Just watch him. See what he does with his ears, eyes, feet, everything."

"Okay. I can do that."

This time, she did.

Sam watched for about twenty minutes. She skipped the snack Gram offered and hurried through her chores. When she returned to the corral, Jake and Mikki were coming out.

Mikki stretched, then shoved her hands in her pockets and looked away from Jake.

"Okay, what did you see?" he asked.

Mikki shrugged.

"Don't interpret, just say what you noticed."

"What's the point, if I don't know what it means?" Mikki shrugged again. "He just stood there."

Sam wished she had a video camera so she could show Mikki herself "just standing there." Besides shrugging and jamming her hands in her pockets, the girl kept her gaze focused over Jake's shoulder. She looked worried, not sassy.

Sam would bet Mikki didn't venture a description because she didn't want to be wrong. She was acting just like the troubled horse inside the corral.

"What about his eyes?" Jake asked.

"Okay," Mikki almost shouted. "He had lines over his eyes, like he was worried, and he didn't like it when I looked right at him." Mikki licked her lips. "He looked away if he caught me staring. Then, when I looked at something else and checked back, he'd be watching *me*. Then the whole thing started over again." Mikki rattled off the words, daring Jake to contradict her. "So what?"

"Anything else?"

"When I moved my hands or feet, just trying to keep them from getting all pins and needly, he scooted away." Mikki looked down. "And that's dumb. He knows he can't get out of there."

"Maybe he doesn't," Sam said.

"What?" Mikki sneered.

"He broke down a fence at the place he used to live," Sam began, then she told Mikki about the snubbing post, the bucking, and the weeks of being ignored.

Mikki listened intently until Sam finished. Then the girl looked frustrated. "So when can I ride him?"

"Not this year," Jake said.

"What?" Again, Mikki's shrill words made Popcorn bolt around the corral. She glanced his way with regret, then plucked at her feathery blond hair. "I can't ride him? Are you afraid I'll screw him up worse?"

"No, we need him to trust someone."

"Like you," Mikki said to Sam. "You're the one reading his mind."

"I'm not reading his mind, just guessing."

"And what do you *guess* it means that he won't let me look into his eyes?" Mikki wagged her head mockingly.

"I think . . ." Sam swallowed and cast a nervous glance at Jake.

This was all his fault. When the Phantom was a foal, Jake had helped Sam think like a horse. She'd never expected to do it aloud.

"I think," Sam said, "that he got everything wrong with people the first time, right after he was captured. Then, instead of trying to understand, they scared him, hurt him, and then shut him out. He wonders why he should try again."

For just an instant, Mikki looked sympathetic,

but then she noticed Jake waiting for her response.

"The reason he should try it *again*"—Mikki pronounced each word slowly, as if Sam weren't very smart—"is because he's a horse. That's what horseys *do*. They give people rides."

"Not wild horses," Sam said.

"He could learn." Mikki flipped her hand toward the corral. "I bet he could learn in a week. You're just teasing me so I'll be a good girl. I've played this game before."

It was quiet for a minute, except for the faraway drone of a small plane overhead. Sam noticed Jake watching it, too.

"See that plane?" Jake nodded toward the cloudless sky and the white trail stretching behind the aircraft.

"Yeah. Why, are you sending me away on one?"

Jake almost smiled. "No," he answered. "Can you fly one?"

"Of course not. Are you crazy?"

"But there's a person flying that plane—"

"A *pilot*," Mikki said in a singsong voice. "Duh."

"A pilot's a human and you're a human." Jake spread his hands out as if he'd explained something simple. "So, you could learn to fly the plane, right? People fly planes. How long do you think it would take you to learn? A week?"

"I'm only eleven years old—"

"Okay," Jake conceded, "so we could give you two weeks."

"I've never done anything like that. You have to learn about wind currents and flaps and—" Mikki stopped, breathless, then closed her eyes. "I get it."

"Three weeks?" Jake teased.

"I said I *get it*, so quit it." Mikki's face flushed.

Sam thought Jake had broken through the girl's cockiness, until Mikki squinted up at him.

"How long till I can ride him?"

Sam gestured toward the sky. "Jake," she muttered, "if I ever, *ever* criticize your patience, remind me of this."

"How long?" Mikki asked again, and Jake recognized the dare.

"When he trusts you," Jake said.

"How will you be able to tell?"

"When he eats out of your hand," Jake began, then shook his head. "No, when he comes to you instead of running away, but you're *not* carrying food." He numbered the first condition off on his index finger, then added, "And when he lets you pet him on the face and neck. Then we can try you on him. Bareback. In this corral."

The gray van that had delivered Mikki just over an hour ago had come to pick her up. As it rolled slowly over the River Bend bridge, Mikki's shoulders sagged.

Before the van parked, though, Mikki started toward it. She didn't say good-bye or thanks or anything, but just before she reached the van she turned back, pointed at Jake and shouted, "You got yourself a deal, cowboy."

## Chapter Eight ⟶

"**I**'D LIKE MIKKI, if she weren't such a brat." Sam watched the gray county van cross the River Bend bridge.

"You would," Jake said, and it wasn't a question.

Sam thought of the way Mikki's shoulders had drooped when she saw the gray van. What was the place like, where the van was taking her? Probably halfway between school and the orphanage in *Annie*, Sam figured, where you didn't get to decide when to study, what to eat, or if you should go for a walk.

It would be a controlled, structured place. Sam wished she could creep inside with her camera and a roll of black-and-white film and show what the girls inside were really like.

"She's got a great vocabulary for a seventh grader," Sam said. "And sometimes she sounds really mature. Do you think that's because she's got a messed-up childhood?"

Jake shrugged.

"Well, *I* think she's intelligent."

"Probably is," Jake said. "But I'm going to tell Wyatt to watch her. She's dangerous."

"Just because she's a smart mouth?"

"I don't think *you're* dangerous," he said. "And you've never been anything but sassy."

Sam stuck out her tongue at Jake, then asked, "But really, what don't you like about her?"

Jake shook his head. "Hard to say. I guess 'cause she's trying to make us think this is no big deal to her." He gestured toward Popcorn. "When it's really the best thing that's happened to her for a long time. She might, I don't know, sort of sabotage herself, and one of the horses might get hurt."

Sam brought Popcorn's food to the round pen while Jake retrieved Witch, his roach-maned black mare, from the barn.

Witch and Popcorn sniffed each other through the panels of the pen, and Witch gave a snorting whinny. Dark Sunshine answered from the barn corral. Sam longed to make the little horse happy.

"If Brynna says it's okay, I want to try everything you're doing with Popcorn on the buckskin."

"Well, that's a fool idea," Jake said.

"Why? I wouldn't do it in the round pen to begin," Sam said. "In fact, I'd leave her where she is, but isolate her from Ace and Sweetheart. What do you think? Maybe she'd start to see me as her herd."

"I won't be part of this," Jake said. "That animal is half scared you're going to put her in the dark, and half scared you'll bring her into the light. You can't trust her to act like a normal horse."

Jake was always too protective, so Sam changed the subject. "Are you going to tell Brynna what you think of Mikki?"

"Don't know. First impression could be wrong, but my gut says it's not."

"They'd probably pull her from the program." Sam heard herself almost defending Mikki, and she couldn't believe it.

"You don't know whether they would or not," Jake scolded. "They didn't send her to another state because she was an angel."

Jake tugged the front of his hat even lower, so Sam couldn't see his eyes. "Anyway, I want Wyatt watching her."

"Since when did you get to be northern Nevada's leading psychologist for humans, too?" Sam was sick of Jake acting superior. Why did he think he was so smart? she wondered. Because he was older, or because he was a guy?

Sam started walking toward the barn corral, and Dark Sunshine must have seen her. The mare's high-pitched neigh split the late-afternoon quiet.

"It doesn't take an expert to diagnose that. Sam, look at her," Jake's voice softened.

As they watched, the tiny mare moved down the

fence and back again, not quite sidestepping, always keeping her face away from them and toward the darkened barn.

"She's—" Jake searched for a word but came up empty.

"Tormented," Sam said. "I'm going to sit with her now."

Jake shook his head. "Do what you want."

"She'll get used to me. She'll see I won't hurt her."

Wordless, Jake gathered his reins, stabbed his boot into Witch's stirrup, and swung aboard. The black danced in place, eager to head for home, but Jake didn't go.

"Sam? Give this some thought. If no one claims that horse and she keeps acting crazy, BLM's going to put her down. I just—" Jake set his jaw as he always did when he'd talked too much, then added, "I don't want you gettin' your heart broke over it."

Sam sat in the shady barn as she had before and studied the mustang. It wasn't easy, with Ace and Sweetheart jostling for Sam's attention.

Sweetheart gave up as soon as she saw Sam's hands were empty, but Ace gave Sam a hooded look meant to make her feel guilty. It did.

Dark Sunshine stayed still. She gazed into the darkness. Beneath her shaggy forelock, Dark Sunshine had a wide forehead and shining brown eyes that expected the worst. Her conformation reminded Sam of Kiger mustangs she'd seen in magazines. Descended from Spanish Barbs, they ran wild in the rugged country surrounding the Kiger River in Oregon.

Brynna said the woman who'd adopted the mare was from Wyoming, but the freeze brand on her neck could say she'd been captured in Oregon.

"You're far from home, aren't you, pretty girl?"

The mare flinched as if Sam had tossed a handful of gravel her way, but she didn't leave. One ear swiveled, listening for trouble, but the other black-edged ear cupped forward to catch Sam's words.

Amazed, Sam kept talking.

"I've got another horse friend who likes it when I talk. His name used to be Blackie. He was my horse." Sam took a breath, and the mare looked over her shoulder. "You saw him the other day, but you were busy having breakfast. You're eating well now, aren't you? And drinking, too. Except for all this crazy stuff, you're doing good, Sunny."

She kept talking. Kigers were supposed to be friendly, but this mare had learned humans meant windowless stalls, whips, and blindfolds.

Those symbols tied Sunshine to men as surely as kindness and his secret name tied the Phantom to Sam.

*Think.* Sam knew she could turn this mare around. It was too late for a secret name. Nothing could make this horse her sister, but maybe they could be friends. Just as she'd won the Phantom's heart after he'd been roped and dragged back to captivity, just as she'd waited in just the right place for Hammer, Sam knew she'd discover the magic to win Dark Sunshine's trust.

"If only horses could give references," Sam said to Jen as they entered the crowded halls of Darton High School the next morning.

"References?" Jen pushed her glasses up her nose and regarded Sam as if she'd lost her mind. "Like when you apply for a job?"

"Sort of." Sam stopped outside her history class. Jen's classroom was right next door, so they could talk until the bell.

"More like a personal reference. If I could get Ace or the Phantom to write Dark Sunshine a letter, she'd understand I'm not going to hurt her."

Jen pressed the back of her hand to Sam's brow. "I think you're coming down with something more serious than my cold, Samantha Anne."

"And I've got the cure," Mrs. Ely said, appearing at the classroom door.

"A healthy dose of history?" Jen asked.

Mrs. Ely laughed, and Sam envied Jen's easy way of balancing the fact that Mrs. Ely was not only a Darton High teacher but also Jake's mom.

Mrs. Ely had known both of them since they were little kids. She was also Sam's history teacher and a talented photographer who encouraged Sam's work with a camera.

"Almost as good as history," Mrs. Ely said. "A photo contest. Jen, you'd better run." She shooed Jen away as the bell rang. "And Sam, talk to me after class."

Sam moved toward her desk, but her way was blocked by Rachel Slocum. Darton High's reigning princess and student body treasurer, Rachel was duly qualified. As Linc Slocum's daughter, she was by far the richest girl in the school.

And the most stylish. Right now, Rachel smoothed a wing of coffee-brown hair away from her eyes, negotiating a deal for last night's homework with a bespectacled boy who could only swallow, hard, as she talked with him.

"I'd be so grateful." Rachel leaned toward him.

One of the advantages of really expensive clothes was that they flowed over you like liquid. At least they did on Rachel. She was wearing some kind of beige outfit that would have looked like a feed sack on Sam, but Rachel looked like she'd stepped out of a fashion magazine.

Sam sat and looked over her shoulder in time to see Rachel leave empty-handed. The guy hadn't given in, and Sam almost applauded. Rachel caught her gloating expression, and Sam could see she was in for it. The last time Rachel had had it in for her, she'd broken the expensive camera signed out to Sam from journalism class. What would she do this time?

Sam took a piece of lined paper from her binder and prepared to take notes. Before Mrs. Ely began talking, though, Sam wrote a note to herself. "Watch your back," it said, and with everything else going on, she vowed to take her own advice.

After class, Sam approached Mrs. Ely's desk. The teacher was handing makeup work to one student and scolding another for gossiping in class, but she slipped Sam a flyer.

The first thing Sam noticed was that the contest wasn't limited to entrants under eighteen. It was open to professional photographers as well as amateurs. She must have looked dubious, because as soon as the others moved toward the door, Mrs. Ely said, "Samantha, that reward you won is as much as some photographers make in a year."

She didn't want to contradict Mrs. Ely, but she sort of had to. "But I earned it under pretty unusual circumstances."

"You did, but your work was fine, and look at the name of the contest. It's perfect for you."

Night Magic, the contest was called. The subject could be anything shot at night, and Sam had once confided to Mrs. Ely that her dream was to photograph wild horses running at night.

"It is perfect," Sam agreed. "But with the, uh, stuff that's going on—" Sam glanced over her shoulder.

Rachel gathered her things in slow motion, eavesdropping. Mrs. Ely nodded that she knew what Sam was talking about. After all, Gram had called Three Ponies Ranch first when she'd been looking for Sam that night.

"The deadline's near Christmas," Mrs. Ely said. "You've got plenty of time."

The warning bell rang in the hall, and Sam jumped like a racehorse in the starting gate.

"I can't be late," she blurted to Mrs. Ely. "If I don't earn all A's in citizenship, I can't ride."

"What a tragedy," Rachel murmured.

Even though Sam beat her to the door, she couldn't shake the feeling she'd given Rachel Slocum one more bit of ammunition to use against her.

Looking like he'd been to town on ranch business, Dad picked Sam up from the bus stop. By the time they reached home, Mikki was already there.

Gram told her Mikki had not only decided to go along with the guidelines for the HARP program, which meant, among other things, keeping a journal about her experiences with the mustangs, but she'd finagled an extension to the time she could spend at River Bend each day.

"Why, she just gobbled up the chocolate chip cookies I gave her, and as soon as Jake arrived, she followed him into the pen," Gram said. "She couldn't wait to see Popcorn."

Sam let her backpack fall to the floor and sat at the kitchen table to devour her own cookies and milk.

"That's great," Sam said, but she didn't exactly mean it. What was wrong with her? Just yesterday, she'd been telling Jake she liked Mikki.

Whatever it was, Popcorn felt it, too.

Out of her school clothes and in riding gear, Sam peered through the slats of the round pen. Yesterday, though he'd stayed far away from Mikki, Popcorn had kept his side turned to her. Today, he was showing her his tail.

*You couldn't fool horses*, Sam thought. Mikki would have to learn that.

Sam wanted to ride Ace. They both needed the exercise. But how could she get Ace out of the barn pen without giving Dark Sunshine a chance to bolt? She'd need to ask Dad for help.

That settled, she left the barn. Blaze met her with a wagging tail. Even he was keeping his distance from Dark Sunshine.

"What's going on with Mikki, huh, Blaze?" Sam rumpled the dog's ears and he whined with pleasure.

Had Mikki made gentling Popcorn a contest against Jake? Had she taken his standards as a challenge? Maybe she was trying to prove something to herself. Or, maybe she thought that if she did a quick job of riding Popcorn, she could take on Dark Sunshine.

"That's not going to happen," Sam muttered to Blaze as the dog walked along with her. "No way."

Blaze wagged his tail and looked up at Sam with openmouthed adoration, believing every word.

## Chapter Nine ∾

$\mathcal{I}$N SAN FRANCISCO, Sam had gone riding twice on rented horses. After the second time, she hadn't wanted to go again. Aunt Sue had worried that Sam was afraid of horses after the accident. Aunt Sue always worried, but she wasn't pushy about it.

"Tell me what you don't like about it," Aunt Sue had said as they drove away from the San Francisco stable for the last time.

Sam had tried. Although she was still a little afraid of falling, Sam could push the fear aside and she told Aunt Sue so. The other part was harder to explain.

Her heart always sank at the end of a ride. Sam hated giving the horse back. She couldn't think of a word to describe the feeling.

"Greed?" Aunt Sue suggested, joking. "Disappointment?"

Together they'd tried, but couldn't come up with it.

Now, Sam didn't have to worry about that feeling.

She rode at a rocking chair lope across the range. With mustang sureness, Ace threaded between clumps of sagebrush. Over his hoofbeats, songbirds sang to the fading afternoon and Sam rode with a joy she'd longed for during those two long years in San Francisco.

To her right lay War Drum Flats and Lost Canyon. To her left, three miles past the blackberry bushes hedging the river, she'd find Three Ponies Ranch, home to Jake's family. Dead ahead, but hours away, the Calico Mountains soared purple against the blue Nevada sky.

Sam knew just where she was, and it was exactly where she wanted to be. She'd do whatever it took to keep the River Bend Ranch. If that meant working with Mikki and doing a good job so they'd win the contract for HARP, she'd cooperate.

Sam had drawn rein to watch a covey of quail rush for cover when she thought she heard someone call her name. She turned, scanned the range, and saw Dad riding Banjo toward her at a walk. Worry swept Sam, until she realized why Dad rode so slowly. Beside him on Gram's pinto, Sweetheart, rode Mikki.

With both hands clamped to the saddle horn, Mikki leaned forward until her forehead almost brushed Sweetheart's mane. Mikki might love horses—the wide smile on her face said as much—

but Sam guessed this was the first time she'd ridden one. Why wasn't Mikki in the round pen with Popcorn? Why wasn't Dad ponying Sweetheart on a lead line? Wasn't he risking a lawsuit or something by letting Mikki leave the ranch yard on horseback?

Dad knew horses better than anyone. If he thought Mikki was safe, Sam wouldn't ask. All the same, she was relieved when Dad explained.

"Jake's been called in to observe the tracking of those rustlers."

"Wow," Sam said. The BLM had federal experts, so this must have been Brynna's idea.

"Kind of an honor for him," Dad said, "but it left Mikki here high and dry. I could've gone in and sat with her, but introducin' a new human to Popcorn so soon isn't fair. I decided to let her try horses from a different angle."

Mikki glanced up. Her expression said she wanted to make a smart-mouth remark, but she was just too happy to think of one. Besides, she sat on Sweetheart as if the pinto were made of eggshell. Mikki must be worried Sweetheart would interpret any move as a command to run.

They rode together, three abreast, until Dad trotted off a short distance to check a water windmill. That's what he said, but Sam knew Dad hoped Mikki would like riding with another kid.

"This is a big deal for Jake, otherwise he wouldn't have left," Sam said.

"I don't care."

Sam's teeth gritted together. So, they were back to that.

"You don't care that he left?" Sam asked her. "Or that it's a big deal for him?"

"Whatever." Mikki stared down at the reins she'd wrapped around the saddle horn. "I don't care."

"He's a really good tracker. His grandfather—"

"Or he just thinks he is," Mikki said.

"No, he's good," Sam insisted. "And he doesn't just do it for pay. Once a local man tried to pay him to track a horse he'd hurt, and he offered Jake a lot of money, but Jake wouldn't do it."

"You leave so many holes in your story, I can tell you're making it up. '*A* local man, *a* horse, *a* lot of money,'" Mikki said. "It's like a commercial on TV: 'many doctors recommend.' Yeah, so who are they?"

Sam didn't know whether to be amused or irritated. "Well, I'm not making it up, and I'm not going to tell you who the man is, though he deserves it, but the horse is the Phantom."

"Yeah, right." Mikki sat back with such emphasis, Sweetheart thought she meant "Whoa," and stopped. "Miss Olson told me that whopper, too. I may not be from around here, but I don't believe in ghost horses."

"He's no ghost." Sam's legs asked Ace to move at a faster walk.

Sweetheart followed without Mikki's urging. When

the pinto and her wobbly rider caught up, Sam glanced at the girl. Mikki bobbed in the saddle, blond hair blowing every which way, but Sam noticed her expression most. Mikki's pointy fox face shone with curiosity. She wanted to know more about the Phantom.

Well, Sam decided, Mikki would just have to wait.

"Jake's tracking those rustlers because they're evil. They hurt Dark Sunshine and trapped those other mustangs to sell for dog food. Right now, they probably have them hidden away, fattening them up so they'll bring more pennies per pound, but they'll kill them soon. And that trap"—Sam gestured toward Lost Canyon—"has been there a while. These are not the first horses they've slaughtered for money."

Mikki attempted to sit straighter in the saddle and hold the saddle horn with only one hand, but she didn't sway with Sweetheart's movements. She lurched.

Putting both hands back on the horn for balance, she asked, "And you don't think Jake's tracking them to get a big reputation?"

Clearly, Mikki had already made up her mind. Sam didn't want to defend Jake. She wanted Mikki to find out for herself, but Sam wasn't that patient.

"Look," she said, "Jake has his faults. For instance, he's obsessed with being my big brother. But he's shy, not a glory hound. He wants to lock up the bad guys. That's all."

Mikki's face turned red. Her hands fidgeted on the reins and Sweetheart's gait turned choppy with confusion.

For the good of the horse, Sam tried to calm Mikki.

"You know, you're trying to teach Popcorn to trust you. Maybe you should learn a little something about it yourself, and admit Jake's a good guy."

"Men are scum!" Mikki shouted, drawing Dad's attention from where he rode ahead of them.

"Not all of them," Sam said, glad the entrance to River Bend had come into view.

"Well, my mom's married three and *they* were all scum. When Miss Olson told me HARP had men teachers, I almost didn't do it. Then, your Dad seemed sort of okay, and you weren't scared—" Mikki cut off the words. "So, isn't that enough *trust* for you?"

Sam swallowed. This conversation was too much for her to handle. Mikki should be talking to someone who knew what she was doing, like a counselor. Or Brynna.

But Sam had no choice, so she did what she'd do if Mikki was a horse. She rewarded this tiny bit of progress.

"You're right. It's trust." She smiled and nodded toward River Bend bridge. "Speaking of trust, I think Sweetheart is starting to like you. Why don't you ride across first. The sound of their hooves on the wood spooks horses sometimes, but I think she'll do it for you."

Mikki crossed alone, not knowing she was more spooked by the sound than Sweetheart, who'd walked over the bridge hundreds of times.

Although Dad rode in behind them and offered to help, Mikki dismounted alone, then walked with wobbly knees to the round pen.

"Is it okay if I open the gate to check Popcorn?" she asked.

Sam glanced at Dad. He nodded.

"Go ahead," Sam said. "And watch him when he first sees you."

Dad stayed on Banjo. He pretended to adjust the gelding's headstall. But Sam wasn't fooled. If Popcorn made a break past Mikki, Dad and Banjo would cut him off.

Mikki emerged from the corral and slid the bolt closed on the gate, looking proud of herself for closing it the right way.

"His head went up and his ears went forward when he saw me," Mikki reported. "He took two steps backward, but he didn't run away. Is that good?"

"In just a couple days? I think that's great," Sam said, but there was no time left to talk. They heard the sound of tires on the desert floor as the gray van drew close, then rolled across the bridge.

Without a good-bye, Mikki trudged toward it.

Sam remembered the feeling of giving back horses at the end of a ride. She still didn't know what it was called, but it felt something like surrender.

If Dad hadn't driven into Alkali for two half gallons of milk, he probably would have called BLM to come get Dark Sunshine.

Left alone to feed the horses, Sam saved Ace, Sweetheart, and the buckskin for last. All three were munching the hay she'd forked to them when Sam gave in to temptation.

Facing into the dark barn, the mare ate. The only sign she even knew Sam was there was the occasional shivering of her skin, as if she were scaring off flies.

Maybe she and Jake and Brynna were all wrong. Maybe the mare's first family had been kind to her, and she only needed to be reminded that the human hand could comfort as well as punish. It was worth a try.

Moving by millimeters, Sam placed one foot on the lowest fence rail, then matched the other beside it. She went up one more rail and leaned out over the top rail, arm extended toward Sunshine's golden hide.

The mustang ran. Ears flat, eyes narrowed, and mouth agape, the mare rushed the fence as if it were invisible. Kicking as she went, the mare collided with the fence. The vibration knocked Sam off the other side of the corral.

Before Sam could stand, before the cloud of dirt and straw could settle, the mare threw herself at the fence again.

*Don't let her get out.*

The rails held, but Sam blamed herself for being an idiot. She'd moved too fast. The mare's trust must be won minute by minute. She needed more than a clumsy reminder that some people weren't monsters.

The mare trembled as if she'd try to batter the rails down with her chest, and her silence was scarier than any scream.

This was no warning. Dark Sunshine's attack wasn't a threat. The mustang's eyes blazed with fear. Sam knew she must be careful. The mare might not be hateful, but flying hooves could kill even if they were used in self-defense.

As Sam turned her back to the corral and walked away, the mare sighed with relief.

Sam rubbed the dust from her eyelashes and stood blinking. Her hands were dirty and she'd only made it worse. Through blurry eyes, she glanced over her shoulder at the mare.

Dark Sunshine's head hung. She breathed short puffs into her hay, but she wasn't eating.

*Poor girl*, Sam thought. *We'll think of something.*

Tomorrow was Thursday. She'd promised to ride up to the trap with Jen. Sam shivered. She didn't want to go back, but maybe Jen could help her find a clue to what those men had done to hurt Dark Sunshine so much.

That night, Sam tossed from her back to her front, tangling her legs in the sheets. She pulled her quilt up and pushed it off.

It was only eleven o'clock, but her brain had been spinning since she'd looked into the mare's eyes. Fear mixed with bravery was a dangerous thing.

Suddenly, Sam sat up.

She knew how to help Dark Sunshine. The Phantom had given her the answer.

How could she help a mustang who only felt safe in the dark? By moonlight.

Phantom had endured terrifying hours with people, and yet he came to her by moonlight. The night he'd taken her to the valley that sheltered his herd, Sam had sat near dozens of wild horses. None had seemed afraid, though they could clearly see her in the brightness of the moon.

It could work. It *would* work!

Sam eased out of bed. Her nightgown swished around her ankles as she crept down the hall to the door of Dad's room. One wooden board creaked under her toes.

"What's wrong?" Dad's voice cut across the sound of bedsprings and his feet hitting his bedroom carpet.

His outline showed in the hall before Sam reached his door.

"I'm sorry. I didn't mean to scare you," Sam managed. He'd sure scared her. Her pulse shook her whole body. "Nothing's wrong."

"You surprised me some. That's all." Dad's tone was calming. "Let's go into your room to talk. I don't want to wake Gram."

Dad followed her back down the hall and switched on the light.

"I wasn't going down to the river." Sam offered the truth as she climbed back into bed. More than once she'd been in trouble for leaving the house at midnight.

Dad nodded. Either he believed her or he was taking in her messy room. He hesitated near the chair piled with boots and jeans, then sat on the bed next to her. For a minute he surveyed the room as if he'd never seen it before.

Dad's fingers brushed the white quilt with the patchwork star, then he stared at her shelf of horse statues, wooden, glass, and plastic. His gaze touched each prancing leg and backswept tail. He studied the unicorn wallpaper just visible inside her closet, and the stack of schoolbooks and magazines about to avalanche off her bedside table.

"I don't blame you for going out there." Dad gestured toward the river. "If I were to blame anyone"— he chuckled—"I guess it would have to be Louise."

Sam held her breath. Louise was her mother, and Dad rarely talked about her. As a child, Sam had asked him about her mother all the time. But her questions so obviously hurt Dad, she'd finally stopped.

Now, he'd just dropped Mom's name between them and laughed at some memory that pleased him.

"She named that river, you know."

"I didn't know!" Sam shook her head. The river had always been called La Charla. She knew it meant "chitchat" in Spanish, and she'd just assumed some lonely explorer had pretended the river's babbling was a voice from home.

"Sure." He nodded. "Before we got married, it was just River Bend's river. But she acted like it was a friend. When she was expecting you, she had a hard time sleeping." Dad gave Sam a sudden smile. "She swore you were doing somersaults inside her. So, she'd slip out of bed and walk down to the river. I don't know how many times I found her there, sitting on a rock, watching the moon dance on the little waves."

Sam's arms wrapped around her ribs. She did the same thing.

"Louise said the sound of the river soothed you, and after she'd sat there a while you'd let her sleep. And then when you were born"—Dad shook his head, as if the rush of memories kept surprising him—"you were a colicky baby. But Louise and I would carry you out in the moonlight and stand by the river, yawning, and it always settled you down so we could grab a nap before you were hungry again."

"I didn't know any of that," Sam said.

"I haven't thought about it for years." Dad's voice changed as he left the past behind. "Just because I don't blame you doesn't mean I think it's safe. Especially now."

"Okay," Sam said. She didn't mind the warning. Dad had just given her a whole new picture of her mother.

Dad cleared his throat and picked up Jingles, the black plush horse that spent his days posed on Sam's pillow.

"What's had you tossing and turning ever since you came in here?" he asked. Dad's index finger touched the gold bells stitched to the toy's saddle. "I figured unless you had ants in your bed, you were stewing about something."

Dad looked up at her then, expecting her to explain.

"I know how to work with Dark Sunshine," she said. "You know how she keeps staring into the barn. I mean, it's natural, since the people who adopted her kept her in a windowless stall."

"Where'd you come by that information?"

"Brynna," Sam said. She hurried, hoping Dad wouldn't point out that Dark Sunshine wasn't there to stay. "And I know how to start gentling her."

"How's that?"

"I could spend Friday night with her in the round corral. We'll put Ace and Sweetheart out in the barn pasture since the fence is fixed, and we'll put Popcorn, alone, in the little corral off the barn."

Dad didn't tell her that she was insane, or that the mare had to go. He just gave Jingles a shake and listened.

"What I'd do is sit with her, then do that herd mirroring thing Jake had me do with Blackie after we'd first weaned him. Remember?"

It was hard to believe the small and scared colt had grown up to be the Phantom, but Sam knew her patient care and attention then had knit the bond that connected them now.

Dad sighed. "Most days it seems a long time since you and that horse were little, but I can still see you in pigtails, following Blackie around when he walked away, then letting him follow you when he needed a leader."

"It worked pretty well, didn't it?" Sam whispered. She wondered if she had her Mom to thank for Dad's unusual patience tonight.

"Yeah, but Blackie was hand-raised, not born wild and abused. One more thing you don't want to forget: Blackie belonged to you."

"Yeah." Sam let the word stretch out.

"I suppose Brynna's mentioned the foster care deal?"

Sam bit her lip. Brynna hadn't. Was Dad talking

about Mikki or Dark Sunshine?

"No, huh? I suppose there's no harm in telling you. She's put through paperwork for us to foster the mare. They do it with orphan foals more often, but there's provisions for adult horses, too. We get paid for helpin' her back to normal."

Sam didn't ask for details, and she didn't bounce on the bed and squeal with joy. She only said, "Oh, wow."

"Someone could still show up with title to that horse," Dad cautioned. "A bill of sale would supersede BLM's agreement with us."

"No one will," Sam insisted. "You know it, Dad. Anyone who's treated her this way doesn't care."

Dad patted her back as if he were searching for words to explain. "Sometimes people want things just to own 'em. It's not fair and it's not right, but they don't know better than to abuse what's theirs. Look at Mikki." Dad shook his head. "That child's had hard use, too."

To Sam, the buckskin was the more likable of the two, but she didn't say it. And the longer she kept her opinion inside, the more clearly she saw how both Mikki and the mare refused to show when they were afraid.

"I guess Mikki's no more to blame for her ugly attitude than Sunshine," Sam admitted.

Dad put Jingles back on the pillow and gave Sam

another pat on the back as he rose.

"Get to sleep, now," he said. "You're going to need lots of energy if you plan to have a slumber party with a wild horse."

## Chapter Ten ❧

"I'M NOT AFRAID of rats or snakes," Sam said. "I just don't like being surprised." Sam hesitated outside the door of the old bus and rubbed her arms free of goose bumps. She couldn't hear anything moving in there, but it looked like a great hiding place for things she'd rather avoid.

Minutes ago, she'd stood in the sunlight that bathed the empty trap at Lost Canyon in autumn gold. Crowded with sagebrush and piñon pine, the old wood had looked picturesque. Only the feed sack cover for the missing truck seemed creepy. She and Jen weren't scared—the place was obviously deserted.

Feeling adventurous, they'd tied their horses at the trap—which was disappointingly free of yellow crime scene tape—and hiked in the direction Sam had seen the cowboy go to retrieve his whip. That's how they'd found the old bus wedged into a narrow chasm.

"Well, I *am* afraid of rats and snakes," Jen admitted suddenly. "Nerve toxins and bubonic plague are things I'd rather enjoy through a microscope."

"The rangers have already been out here, and they probably disturbed whatever animals were living inside," Sam reasoned.

Jen gave Sam a lopsided smile. "Oh, good. Now they're ticked off and ready to protect their home."

Sam considered the bus again. Painted a pale blue that had faded almost to white, it was obviously not a school bus. Jen had suggested it was a prison bus for shuttling convicts between jail and work crew chores. Whatever its former purpose, someone had positioned it in this natural niche so that the windows on one side were smack against the hillside. The side she and Jen could see was creased and rusty.

They'd thought it was long abandoned, until Jen noticed clothes tucked into windows in place of curtains and Sam saw the path worn to the door, which was folded halfway open.

"Okay, we don't have to go in," Sam said.

"Of course we do," Jen said. "The rustlers probably holed up here between horse trappings. We might find something the rangers overlooked."

"Not likely."

"But possible," Jen insisted. "It'd be great if we found something with a name on it."

"Oh, and how about an address, too?" Sam said. "A driver's license would be good. Then the rangers could just cruise over and pick them up."

"You're getting as sarcastic as me," Jen said, crossing her arms. "So knock it off. I just want the rustlers caught so that you don't have to keep looking over your shoulder all the time. Which reminds me . . ."

"Yes?" Sam couldn't help looking back down the canyon toward the trap.

"Does your dad know where you are?"

"He wasn't home. He doesn't get a half day off like we do. And I told Gram I was going riding with you." Sam smiled, but Jen's implication gave her chills.

"So no one knows where we are." Jen gave her voice a ghost story waver.

"Who did you expect me to tell—Jake?"

"No. Definitely no." Jen squared off, facing the bus door, then tugged Sam's shirtsleeve. "After you, Nancy Drew."

Sam pushed the door open the rest of the way and jogged up the stairs. Something *did* skitter inside, but Sam was more aware of the odor.

"Yuck, it smells like old sweaty socks." She grimaced.

"Mixed with a lingering aroma of canned chili." Jen moved ahead of Sam and nodded to tin cans scattered under a blanket-covered bus bench.

They both looked down the aisle. It was clear, almost as if it had been swept, but some seats leaned at weird angles and several had come unbolted from the floor.

Sam was wondering if the bus had rolled down there from the highway, when Jen took a squeaky breath and pointed.

"Behind you."

Sam whirled, gasping.

And saw nothing.

"Ow! You stomped on me!" Jen complained.

"Serves you right." Sam panted. "What are you looking at? I don't see anything." Sam scanned the driver's seat, the speedometer, a sun-cracked plastic frame where the driver's license was supposed to go.

"That," Jen said.

On the shallow shelf below the driver's mirror, Sam finally saw what Jen had spotted.

An empty cottage cheese carton held water with something floating on the top. It wasn't cottage cheese. Next to the carton sat a man's razor with gross bits of whisker still clinging to it.

Jen edged past Sam for a closer look.

She was welcome to it, Sam thought as she backed away and started back down the center aisle. This was ridiculous. What did they think they were going to find?

Sam looked to her right. A seat held two sleeping bags, one ripped with fluffy stuff poking out. She looked left. A coiled rope hung over a seat back and a glove lay on the bench part.

The floor slanted beneath her feet. The bus must have a flat tire on this side. Sam started to grab a seat back for balance, when Jen's voice startled her again.

"Don't touch anything," Jen said. "Just in case they haven't fingerprinted."

"You watch too much television," Sam grumbled.

That's when a shiny mouse ran over her left boot toe and ducked under the jean hem on her right leg.

"Oh, no!" Sam bawled.

She stamped. The mouse fell.

He scurried back the way he'd come. Sam shuffled and scooted her feet, trying not to crush him. Her foot slid out from under her and she stumbled, landing facedown.

"Don't touch anything!" Jen yelled again.

"Tell that to the paramedics when they arrive," Sam mumbled.

Jen moaned, and Sam felt her friend's footsteps pound closer. She'd frightened Jen, and that wasn't very nice. But Sam wasn't feeling nice. She lay in the aisle of this convict bus, with the breath knocked from her chest. She needed to do a push-up to get upright, but she didn't like the idea of pressing her bare hands against this floor.

From her position, she saw the undersides of seats. No gum, just cobwebs and red-brown rust where a metal seat support had cracked, showing a corner of yellow paper.

Sam closed her eyes, then opened them.

"Are you okay? Sam, do you have a concussion or something?" Jen squatted nearby.

"I see something?"

Jen sat quiet for a minute. "Why are you asking me? Sam, you'd better be all right. I can't carry you down to—"

"You don't have to." Sam flipped into a seated position before she delicately removed a piece of paper that had been rolled and slipped inside the metal tube.

"Oh, wow." Jen sighed, and they read it together.

Sold for $125 and barter goods
1 bukskin mere,
3yrs old and tack
to Certis Flickinger

"I can't read the signature," Jen said, "but this guy needs some help in English."

Sam read the words again.

"It's signed by Rose Bloom. See the *B* there? She's the lady who adopted Dark Sunshine and got title to her a few months ago. That's what Brynna said."

This bill of sale proved Dark Sunshine belonged to someone named Certis Flickinger. He had to be one of the rustlers.

"What are you going to do?" Jen asked, and Sam

wanted to hug her. This is what made Jen a best friend.

Jen wouldn't give advice until she was asked. They both knew they should turn the bill of sale over to someone in authority, and they both knew the horse would suffer even more if they did.

"What do you think?" Sam asked.

"I think that looks like a carbon copy," Jen said, "and Rose Bloom has the original, so you can't keep it a secret forever."

"I wouldn't do that." Sam folded the yellow paper into a square and tucked it inside her front pocket. "But I do want to think about it a little while."

Sam checked Jen's expression. Inside a frame of blond braids, Jen's face had turned serious. Jen was a math whiz with a knack for logical, well-ordered thinking. If there was a flaw in waiting, Jen's analytical mind would find it.

Outside, a breeze blew and a branch of sagebrush tapped against the bus. Finally, Jen shook her head.

"Other than the tiny chance we're being watched right now by federal rangers—and I think Ace and Silly would have let us know if they'd sensed them— I see no problem with waiting." Jen rubbed her hands together and stared at them, still thinking. "After all, we are juveniles . . ."

"And we can't be expected to know this is important?" Sam suggested.

"They're not going to buy that, Samantha Anne.

Otherwise, why would we take it?"

"You're right." Sam ignored Jen's gesture that said *as usual.* "Let's get out of here. I'm supposed to be home in time to help Jake with Mikki."

Leading the way back to the door, Jen said, "Just don't tell Jake."

"Not in this lifetime," Sam promised. But by the time they'd made their way off the bus and back to the horses, Sam thought she might ask Jake what he'd overheard when he was hanging out with the official trackers.

After all, it couldn't hurt.


Sam reined Ace aside and waited for the gray van to cross the River Bend bridge. Even from there, she heard Dark Sunshine's worried whinny.

As Sam rode into the ranch yard, she saw why.

Far back by the barn, Jake stood between Witch and Sweetheart. With Sam on Ace and Sweetheart outside the barn corral, Dark Sunshine felt abandoned by her new herd.

Right in front of Sam was another surprise. Mikki, who'd just arrived, was talking with Pepper.

Mikki wore jeans and a black tee shirt stenciled with the word "Misfit." Whether it was the name of a band or a description of the wearer, Mikki had better be nice to Pepper.

Sam shook her head at her own silliness. Why should she feel protective of a cowboy talking to an eleven-year-old girl?

Because she really liked him. Pepper, with his red-blond hair and gangly legs, was only seventeen, but he wasn't quiet like Dallas or Ross, River Bend's other hands. He didn't offer Sam extra care because she was the boss's daughter or scoff because she'd been a city girl.

Pepper just accepted Sam. His winks, nods, and the stampede string he'd made for her hat had kept Sam's spirits high while she was relearning her place at home.

As Sam rode close enough to eavesdrop, she heard Mikki ask why Pepper had become a cowboy.

"No choice," Pepper said with a slow smile.

"What does that mean?" Mikki demanded.

"I'm too lazy to work and too nervous to steal," Pepper answered.

Mikki laughed, but Sam winced with uneasiness. The bill of sale in her pocket and the technically stolen horse in a River Bend corral might make her a thief, but Pepper shouldn't be joking with Mikki about stealing.

But hadn't Mikki been a runaway? Pepper had been, too, when he'd first come to the ranch. Maybe he and Mikki could find things in common.

Before she dismounted to join in the conversation, Sam saw Jake hailing her from the barn.

Sam rode back to him. Jake was already dusty, as

if he'd been working. He'd loosened Witch's cinch, too, so the horse could relax.

Sweetheart was saddled. Had Jake used his half day off to work while she'd gone riding with Jen?

"I've been working with Popcorn," he said. "I've got him haltered."

"Jake, that's great."

He shrugged. "It's the horse, not me. He's sweet as pie." Then Jake's mouth twisted in irritation. "She probably *will* ride him before she leaves."

Looking embarrassed, Jake changed the subject. "Leave Ace tacked up so you can help me switch the buckskin and Popcorn after she's done working with him."

Sam noticed that Jake had avoided using Mikki's name.

"You still feel uneasy about her," Sam said.

"I arranged for the van driver to come back late so she could make some real progress today." He sounded a little defensive.

"But you still don't trust her, right?" Sam asked.

"I won't talk about it."

Sam took a breath, then let it go. "How about your tracking trip? Will you talk about that?"

Jake's face lit with a rare smile. "Later," he promised, and began walking toward the round pen.

"What, are you like a cop-in-training now?" she teased.

"Later." Jake shot Sam a look meant to silence her. It didn't work.

"Jake, was it really cool? Tell me."

"If I *were* training as a cop, first thing I'd do is put you under house arrest."

"I haven't done anything!" Sam felt a zing of worry.

There was no way Jake could know what was in her pocket.

"Unless your fool idea of spending the night with that mare counts." At her silence, Jake looked smug. "Your dad called and told me about it this morning while you were waiting at the bus stop."

Jake never missed a chance to gloat. While it took Sam over an hour to reach Darton High on the bus, he made it in half that time, driving in with his brother.

All of a sudden, that didn't matter. Sam had to know if she was rushing Dark Sunshine. If her idea was a mistake, Jake would tell her.

"Jake." She grabbed his forearm, tightening her grip when he tried to shake her off. "I'm only going to keep Sunny company in the dark and mirror her movements, like you taught me. That's all. What do you think? Really."

Sam released Jake's arm. He looked down, then rubbed the back of his neck in a thoughtful gesture.

"I think it's a good idea for the horse," he said. "I'm not so sure about you."

"You know I'm careful around horses."

"Bloody noses and black eyes. Shoot, now." Jake pretended to frown in confusion. "Who *was* that I saw, if not you?"

Sam was sticking her tongue out at Jake when she felt Mikki's stare. Maybe it would be good for Mikki to see it was possible to disagree with a man and not fight.

Mikki turned on her heel, away from Pepper. She pretended she hadn't been watching Sam and Jake at all, and started toward the round pen.

"Just a second," Jake called. "Before we go in, I want to tell ya what we're doing. It's different." Jake ignored the girl's loud sigh and tapping foot. "You're going to make a deal with Popcorn."

"A deal?"

"Yeah, if he doesn't run from you, you won't chase him. It's that simple. Sam, show her." Jake motioned her closer. "You be the horse."

"Oh, good." Sam tossed her hair, pretending it was a mane, then walked away. Jake followed. "If I were a mustang," Sam called back to Mikki, "this would make me nervous, especially when he speeds up like that."

Sam and Jake speed-walked in a circle. When Jake stopped, Sam slowed down to watch him. As soon as she faced him, Jake retreated a step.

"But you're letting the horse back you down," Mikki said.

"It looks like it, at first, but pretty soon you'll have him coming to you—to eat, to get haltered—"

"To ride," Mikki interrupted. "Okay, I understand, but that'll take hours."

"If you're lucky," Jake agreed.

"Why not just rope him, pull him over, then hold him and pet him until he knows I'm not going to hurt him?" Mikki said.

"That wouldn't work for me," Sam said. "If some creature tied me up and dragged me somewhere, then wanted to touch my head, I'd fight to get away, wouldn't you?"

"There she goes again, thinking like a horse," Jake said.

A blush heated Sam's cheeks from this best of all compliments, but the real warmth came from inside. Jake's praise meant a lot.

"That's not fair. It comes natural to her. She's been on a horse every day of her life. I just got here."

"Sam can think like a horse because she pays attention. And she cares about horses," Jake corrected. "If you're nice, Sam might tell you where she's really been these last two years." Mikki didn't take the bait, only asked, "Okay, what are Sam Forster's rules to thinking like a horse?"

*Why should I tell you?* Sam squashed the thought. She'd act like an adult while Mikki played the bratty little kid.

"There are really only a few rules you'll need to be

a horse today," Sam said. "One: The herd is where you're safe. Two: Run from anything that might hurt you."

"Don't I get to play?" Pepper joked as he moved closer, reminding them he was still there.

"That's it?" Mikki ignored him and moved toward the gate.

"That's it." Jake walked after her. "Now, you'd better get to work, because we're moving Popcorn to another corral today, and you"—he pointed at Mikki—"are going to lead him there."

## Chapter Eleven ॐ

JAKE'S PLAN WORKED perfectly. For a half hour, Mikki walked and talked with Popcorn as if she were one of his kind. During the second half hour, she did the same, except she held the end of a long rope attached to his halter. At last, Popcorn followed Mikki wherever she went.

"Just keep walking as long as you hear his hooves behind you," Jake told Mikki. "And don't look back."

"How far away is he?" Mikki asked as she walked past Jake.

"He's staying a good seven or eight feet back. That's his flight distance. He knows you can't grab him from there."

Peering into the corral, Sam noticed Mikki's smile. Right now, the girl wasn't trying to prove she was tough. She wasn't acting like she didn't care. She'd spoken Popcorn's language and told him he could trust her. She was proud of something that mattered.

"I wish my mom could see this," Mikki said as she passed Jake again.

"Maybe she can in a few weeks," he said casually. "I'm sure she'd be welcome."

Finally, it was time to take Popcorn outside the round pen and move Dark Sunshine into it.

Jake bolted the front gate, just in case something went wrong. Pepper walked out to the gate with Jake. Though he talked loudly enough for the girls to hear, Sam had the feeling something else was going on.

"I think Mikki can handle Popcorn, but I don't know what to expect from the mare," Jake said.

Mikki left the round pen with Popcorn. The albino's head swung toward the ten-acre pasture, toward the barn, and though he picked his feet up high, showing he was nervous, he followed Mikki to an open spot near the house.

"Good," Jake said to Mikki. Then, Jake nodded to Pepper as he settled on the front porch with Gram.

Everyone was watching.

"I'll put two loops on the buckskin," Jake told Sam. "You hold one and I'll take the other. We'll keep her kind of cross-tied between Ace and Sweetheart. They're her herd now, so maybe she won't put up a fuss till we get to the round pen."

"She won't like that." Sam considered the pen as if she were Dark Sunshine. Would the mare remember the buzzing motorcycles, whooping men, and mustangs running into a trap?

"When we get her as far as the open gate, you'll ride Ace in and I'll release my rope. I think she'll follow."

Sam sized up the entrance to the pen. Blindfolded, the mare had followed Ace all the way to the River Bend. This might work.

"I talked it over with Wyatt," Jake said. "This is the best we could come up with."

"Let's go," Sam said.

Jake made a bow to Mikki, Pepper, and Gram. "This rodeo won't last too long," he promised.

Jake lassoed Dark Sunshine with such gentleness, she looked confused. Only when Sweetheart and Ace tugged her away from the dark barn did she snort in alarm.

Jake and Sam let the horses work the ropes as the buckskin tossed her head, trying to flip off the loops around her neck.

Sam found it hard to stay quiet, but her voice wouldn't soothe the mare. Maybe this time tomorrow, but not yet.

The mare rocked back, pawed in a half rear, then landed on four stiff legs. She trotted, black mane fanning on one side, then the other, as she looked from Ace to Sweetheart. Hopping and blinking against the sun, Dark Sunshine was nearly to the round pen when Mikki yelled.

"Popcorn, no! You're not going anywhere!"

After that, Sam only heard pounding hooves and Sunshine's screams. The mare reared so high, Sam feared she'd fall over backward. Ace and Sweetheart barely kept her earthbound.

Body thrashing, head slinging, the mare might have escaped, except that River Bend cow ponies were the best. Ace and Sweetheart had been schooled to sidestep charging steers and stay calm in the midst of stampedes. Tails swishing, they kept plodding toward the round pen.

"No! Oh, no, you don't!" Mikki's shrill voice rose loud enough for Sam to hear it, but she couldn't imagine what had gone wrong.

She didn't try. Her job was to get Dark Sunshine into the corral. Pepper and Gram would have to help Mikki.

Just ahead, the round pen gate stood open. Sam leaned low on her gelding's neck.

"C'mon, Ace, lead her in," she whispered.

Ace leaped forward, passed the mare, and entered the round pen. Ropes dropped loose, swarming around his legs, but Ace ignored them. Even when the gate slammed, Ace listened to Sam's hands and loped around the pen, with the mare right behind.

After several laps around the pen, Jake opened the gate so Sam could ride Ace through. But Jake had never seen the mare's need to stay with her herd. She would not be left behind.

Head level, ears pinned so flat they were lost in

the torrents of black mane, Dark Sunshine pressed close to Ace, joining his charge for the gate.

Before they got there, Jake slammed the gate. He stood in his stirrups to shout over the fence.

"Ditch Ace and climb over," Jake said. Then he vanished.

It wasn't that hard. If her hands hadn't been shaking, Sam could have stepped off Ace and grabbed the fence in one fluid movement.

But Sam was afraid to see what was happening outside the round pen. When she did, she wanted to give Mikki a shake.

Popcorn was trying to behave. He rushed toward Mikki as she stepped back, but the sight of five hundred pounds of horse coming at her made Mikki panic.

"No! No!" Mikki screamed at the gelding, jerking his head with the halter rope. She tried to make him stop, but he thought the pulls meant "Come closer."

At last, Jake signaled Pepper to move in. The young cowboy stepped between the girl and horse, slipped the rope from her hands, and gave her a gentle shove back.

*Oh, boy. Mikki didn't like that*, Sam thought. But Pepper's concern was for the frightened albino.

At the end of the lead rope, Popcorn flailed with his front hooves, trying to break loose and run. Pepper hunkered down on his boot heels. He kept his weight low, so the horse couldn't jerk him off his feet and drag him.

Finally, sweat-darkened and breathless, the gelding stood still and waited.

Pepper straightened his knees. Gradually, crooning and talking, he walked to the horse. Lazily, he coiled the rope, until he was just feet away.

"Hey, Jake," Pepper said, "what d'you say I walk this fella back to the barn corral?" With a calm stride, Pepper moved away and Popcorn followed.

The albino's willingness, after such a battle, made Sam so mad at Mikki she didn't know what to say to her.

Gram was always sensible and straightforward — she should go over and lecture Mikki. But Jake snatched the job.

Without looking at Sam, he handed her Sweetheart's reins and then his hat.

What in the world? Sam looked down at the dusty Stetson and wondered what it signified.

Jake jerked the rawhide tie from his hair, then reknotted it. Even though Jake's breathing had slowed by the time he walked up to Mikki, Sam wished Gram would step between them.

Mikki looked around frantically, as if she were being bullied, but Gram stayed on the porch.

"Look, it's not my fault!" Mikki shouted. "Popcorn started being a jerk. He ran right at me. He tried to trample me. He just . . . well . . . I . . ."

Jake let her protests run down.

"Horses can be scared or pushy," he said. "They cannot be jerks."

"He was trying to act all tough—"

This time Jake interrupted. "He *is* tough. He's bigger and stronger than you are. Fighting won't work. It might've made other kids or your mom do what you wanted, but it won't work with a horse. A horse has to trust you, and Popcorn was well on his way. He got scared and turned to you. He needed his herd leader—*you*—to be strong."

Jake waited for Mikki to meet his eyes. When she did, he wasn't easy on her.

"You let him down, girl. You panicked. What's he supposed to think if you've been saying 'Trust me and I'll take care of you,' then you yell at him, yank him around, and prove you're weak?"

Mikki looked small. Her defiance was gone. Both hands covered her mouth, as if that would somehow smother Jake's words.

Sam watched the two. Jake didn't trust Mikki, but he'd had enough confidence in her that her actions had disappointed him. Mikki didn't like Jake, and yet she was shrinking with shame.

When the gray county van honked at the gate, Sam ran to open it. As it drove in, Pepper walked from the barn corral toward Mikki. At first, his head was cocked to one side, as if he were explaining something.

Sam couldn't hear what Mikki said to him, but Pepper recoiled and his voice carried across the yard.

"I'll tell you one thing," Pepper snapped. "On this ranch, ladies don't talk that way." His index finger stabbed in her direction. "No, nor guys, neither!"

"Then maybe I just won't come back to this stupid ranch!" Mikki shouted. She ran toward the van, bumped into the side of it, and pounded on the door until it opened.

Pepper looked stunned. "I'm sorry, Jake," he said as the van rolled away. "It's not my job to scold her." He rubbed his palms on the front of his jeans. "Shoot, Sam, if I've wrecked this program for you all, after everyone's been so good to me, I just don't know what I'll do."

Jake clapped a hand on Pepper's shoulder.

"She deserved it, and she's tough enough to take it," Jake said. "She'll be back. That kid has some major problems, but she's no quitter."

Sam nearly fell asleep in the bathtub. Her head started off propped against the tile. Bit by bit, she slipped down until the water was lapping at her lips.

Warm water soothed muscles knotted by her fall in that creepy bus and from the buckskin throwing her weight against the rope.

The aromas of chicken soup and fresh-baked bread wafted up the stairs. Dinner would be ready when she went down.

Spending all night in the corral didn't seem like such a good idea anymore. Sam's eyelids drooped. She might have dozed if her gaze hadn't stopped on the jeans she'd tossed on the floor. One pocket held Dark Sunshine's bill of sale. Sam's eyes sprang wide open.

She pulled the plug from the bathtub, wrapped a towel around herself, ran shivering to her room, and hid the bill of sale inside a sock in her bottom drawer.

She knew she had to inform Brynna about the bill of sale. But she wouldn't do it tonight.

When she left the warm kitchen for the round pen, Sam hardly noticed the temperature difference. For her slumber party with Dark Sunshine, she wore thermal underwear, jeans, a long-sleeved shirt covered by a jacket, gloves, and a knit cap.

She also brought snacks. A can of sweet grain for the mare, a candy bar for herself.

The sun had set when she opened the gate, but dusk still lingered. Jake had managed to slip Ace out of the round pen. Now, disturbed by another human invasion, Dark Sunshine trotted away. She circled the pen until she neared Sam, then wheeled and ran in the opposite direction, shaking her head fiercely because, once again, Sam didn't retreat.

"I'm not scared of you, pretty girl."

To make herself smaller and less threatening, Sam sat in the dirt with her back against the fence.

The buckskin didn't know what to make of that. She kept shaking her mane, though her hooves moved in a regular beat. It didn't take Sam long to hear eight separate hoof falls, followed by hesitation, and then eight more steps.

Suddenly, Dark Sunshine changed her path. She galloped along the fence, until Sam's nearness made her veer through the middle of the pen. Instead of circles, she made ovals. Over and over again.

Dusk had turned to darkness when the mare stopped.

"That didn't take long," Sam said. Though she could see only the mare's outline, Sam heard her tail swish. "Ready to come over and have a little grain?"

Since it was too soon to ask the mare to take it from her hand, Sam used a scoop. She jiggled it to waft the scent toward the buckskin.

With a snort, Dark Sunshine began trotting ovals again.

"As if you'd fall for such a trick." Sam laughed. "Is that what you're telling me?"

Next, Sam tried the technique Mikki had used on Popcorn.

"Keep walking away and I'll follow you," Sam explained to the mare. "Stop and I'll stop. Take one step toward me and I'll back up."

The mare uttered an insulted grunt, then resumed trotting around the corral with Sam right behind her.

After an hour, Sam yawned.

"Do what you want. I'm taking a break." Sam stopped and the buckskin stopped, too, blowing a sigh through her lips.

*Energy. I need energy.*

Sam looked at her watch. It was 12:07. She felt hot and queasy, and it was hours until dawn. She took the candy bar from her pocket. The mare's ears twitched at the crinkling wrapper.

"I'll share," Sam coaxed. "C'mon, Sunny." She smooched at the mare. "No girl can refuse chocolate."

The mare looked the other way, lifting her chin as if something far more interesting were happening outside the corral.

"We're making progress, even if you won't admit it," Sam told the mare.

Quietly, Sam mimicked a nicker. Clearly, the horse didn't recognize it. Instead of pricking her ears forward, she let them fall to the sides.

"It wasn't so bad that you have to give me the mule look." Sam yawned again. "You know you're exhausted, so how 'bout just one step this way?"

As if she understood, the contrary mare backed a few steps.

"Show-off," Sam said. "I'm coming after you."

Sam's steps were sluggish. She glanced at her watch as she chased the mare: 12:12. Five minutes had passed like an hour. She had to do something to wake up.

She could stick her head in a horse trough. That

would wake her, but it was a little gross, even for a girl who loved horses. If she went inside for a cold shower, she'd wake Dad and Gram. That left the river.

La Charla whispered to Sam. This time of year the river was low. After running over sun-warmed rocks all day, it shouldn't be too cold, even though the night air was chilly.

Sam slipped through the round pen gate and locked it behind her. Dark Sunshine gave a low whinny that probably meant "Good riddance."

"I'll be back," Sam called to her. "This party won't be over for hours."

The porch light and full moon lit the path to the river. Once she reached it, Sam sat on a rock and thought of her mother doing the same.

Then, before her thoughts turned dreamy, Sam tugged off her boots. She left them on the shore. Sucking in a breath, avoiding unsteady stones, Sam waded out.

An owl hooted nearby. Up to her knees, Sam stayed on one side of a big rock streaked with quartz. It blocked the river's rills and formed a tiny pond within the river. Its surface was satiny and smooth enough to reflect the moon.

Tonight's moon wore a halo of rose-gold mist, and it floated right there at her feet.

Hadn't she read about ancient people who stared into still pools to tell the future? Sam wished she knew how. What was the meaning of a haloed moon and a handful of stars?

Dizziness made her stumble forward. She caught herself before her knees hit the water, and she pushed herself up, planted her feet, and rubbed her eyes. The huge splash had silenced the owl. Sam was tempted to stand in the darkness, letting the murmuring waters lull her, but she was making progress with the buckskin and she needed to get back.

Drawing a deep breath, Sam tried one more time to tell her future. She looked into the pool. What she saw surprised her so much she didn't even gasp.

Another face was reflected next to hers.

## Chapter Twelve ∞

THE PHANTOM GLOWED on the river's surface. As Sam looked up from the reflection, so did he, greeting her with a nicker so quiet only his nostrils quivered.

Sam wanted to hug him. Memory promised his neck would be warm and solid in the circle of her arms, but she stayed patient.

"Zanzibar," she whispered.

Three times the stallion bowed his head. With each nod, his forelock flipped up, sifted down. When the forelock parted the third time, his eyes shone with mischief. A second later, he splashed closer. His head snapped down, then up. If she hadn't known the game, Sam might have thought the feathery touch was a whisper of wind over her hand.

It wasn't. Years ago, Sam and the stallion had played a game she called "nibbles." In it, the colt darted close, swung his muzzle her way, and gently lipped her hand before trotting off, pretending it had never happened.

"You're teaching that horse to bite," Dad had told her, but the colt never did.

Why had the Phantom remembered the game now? Why did this mighty stallion frolic around her like a dog? Flicking her hand through the air, Sam teased him, but she was also careful to dodge the stallion's rough moves. He couldn't know her skin was thinner than his hide.

As Dark Sunshine's neigh soared through the night, the stallion stopped. Head held high, he interpreted the mare's cry, then lowered his head and considered the girl before him. The Phantom had many mares, but Sam was the only human he loved.

She saw him decide to stay with her, and hoped no one woke to investigate Dark Sunshine's neighs.

Moments with the Phantom were hers alone. Sam knew he'd run at the approach of another human. He could carry himself to safety, but she didn't want anyone else to see him vanish like a ghost up the hillside.

*Face it*, Sam thought, *you don't want anyone else to lay eyes on him.*

For two years, Sam and the colt had longed for each other. Once she returned, nothing could keep them apart.

Sam held out her hand, palm up. The Phantom buried his muzzle in the cup of her hand, but he didn't continue the game. He pressed down, then drew his chin toward his chest, urging Sam to move closer. She did.

Her other hand combed through his mane. Each time her fingers hit a snag, she untangled it.

Watchfulness vibrated through the stallion, but he wanted the grooming and didn't mind the tugging of her fingers.

Since he hadn't been brushed in two and a half years, strands of mane pulled loose, and suddenly Sam had an idea.

Once before, she'd thought that what she really needed to tame Dark Sunshine was a recommendation from another wild horse. Maybe Zanzibar could give it to her.

Each time a long thread of hair worked free, Sam tucked it into her pocket. She'd braid a horsehair bracelet, a silver token to wear beside the black one she'd made from her colt's mane years ago. The untamed scent might tell Dark Sunshine that Sam could be trusted.

As she tucked more strands into her pocket, she looked down. The moon was still bouncing along the surface of the river when the image shattered.

They had company.

The click of the border collie's toenails on the bridge alerted the horse to Blaze's approach, and the stallion leaped, front feet tucked up like a carousel horse.

As the Phantom dashed to the distant shore, Sam ran for the ranch.

"Stay, Blaze, stay," she called. She could see his silhouette on the bridge. She had to keep him from barking.

Hours ago, Blaze had bedded down in the bunkhouse, so he must have scratched at the door long enough that someone had gotten up to let him out. That meant one of the cowboys could be up and walking around in the darkness.

Breathless, Sam paused on the bridge and looked around. The dog seemed to be alone. He growled and bristled, staring into the night, but the Phantom had vanished.

"You crazy dog." Sam rubbed Blaze's ears.

At her touch, he shed his fierce stare and gazed up at her, openmouthed and happy. He bounced along beside Sam until she reached the round pen. Then he sauntered to the house, climbed the front porch steps, and threw himself down to sleep.

Sam wanted to do the same. Instead, she entered the pen. Dark Sunshine moved away, but she didn't slam against the slats as she had before.

"You're not trying to ram your way out, are you, girl?" Sam leaned against the fence, then slid down until she was sitting in the dirt.

The mare watched, waiting for Sam to get up and chase her. But Sam only yawned.

"You're gonna have to get used to me like this," she said.

Before another ten minutes passed, Sam was sound asleep.

Something told her not to open her eyes, not to gasp, not to jerk away from whatever was moving nearby.

Sam stayed still. It wasn't the early-morning chill that had wakened her. Sam heard snuffling and smelled the sweet dusty scent of horse. Then she felt a bump against her denim-covered hipbone.

Dark Sunshine was nuzzling her pocket.

Sam lifted her eyelids just enough to see a stretch of buckskin neck. The mare startled back a step. Her black-tinged ears tilted toward Sam, but when Sam didn't move, the mustang's muzzle returned. She was sniffing the pocket where Sam had stashed the Phantom's hair.

The nudging tickled, and finally Sam couldn't help laughing. When she did, Sunny trotted off a few steps, but she tilted her head, still looking curious.

"That's it." Sam stood and walked toward the gate.

As she glanced back, Sam saw the mare wearing the expression she'd been waiting for. If Dark Sunshine was curious, if she didn't want Sam to leave until she'd discovered what was in her pocket, that was good.

Outside the gate, Sam didn't stop to roll the stiffness from her shoulders. She hurried toward the house, thinking of bed.

In the entire history of River Bend Ranch, no one had been allowed to sleep until noon, and Sam was no exception. In fact, this was one of the busiest Saturdays Sam could remember. Ross, Pepper, and Dallas had gone over early to the Gold Dust Ranch to help unload Slocum's new Brahma breeding stock.

Sam had already put in a full day of work when Brynna arrived with Mikki at two o'clock.

At the sound of the white BLM truck, Sam looked out the kitchen window. Mikki climbed out. Arms crossed, she walked a few stiff steps, as if her legs were sticks.

"Look at her," Sam said to Gram. "She doesn't want to be here, and she sure doesn't look sorry."

Gram didn't look up from the cheese she was shredding for that night's taco dinner. "Who should she apologize to, the horse?"

"How can you feel sorry for her, Gram? After she jerked poor Popcorn around and just"—Sam swept her hand through the air—"threw away the trust he put in her?"

Gram flashed Sam a disappointed look. "I feel sorry for her because she was scared, and she failed at something she was about to get good at, something that matters to her very much."

"She sure doesn't act like it matters." Sam heard her childish tone even before Gram spoke.

"Samantha, for a girl who's so good at reading animals, you are downright dense when it comes to human beings."

"I probably am, but—" Sam stopped. She'd been about to point out Mikki's baggy jeans and frazzled blond hair, but she stopped just in time.

"You think that horse's trust has been betrayed?" Gram slammed the cheese grater on the counter. "Mikki's mother has married three men and—if Mikki's right—each time she's put the man before her child."

Sam stared at the whitewashed kitchen ceiling, trying to keep tears from overflowing. Her own mother had died and left her behind, but not because she wanted to go.

"Honey, can't you see why Mikki doesn't show her feelings? Can't you recognize a heart that's been broken one too many times?"

Sam swallowed hard, then cleared her throat. "If Popcorn will give her a second chance, so will I," Sam said. It was only for an hour. She could do it. "And if Popcorn is cranky, I'll help her make up with him."

Gram put her work aside and wrapped Sam in a hug. Sam shut her eyes, enjoying the closeness Mikki would envy.

"Used to be, I could kiss the top of your head when I hugged you," Gram said. "Now you're just getting too big." Gram gave her a loud kiss on the cheek. "You're a good girl, Samantha, just a little impatient. But you'll have a chance to practice: Mikki and Brynna are joining us for dinner tonight."

Popcorn gave Mikki a second chance, and Sam practiced patience. Since Jake was in Darton, helping his mom with the week's shopping, Sam took over.

The busy morning had become a quiet afternoon. After Dallas, Ross, and Pepper had helped Slocum with his Brahmas they'd gone to town together. As they were backing Dallas's truck around to leave, even Blaze had jumped in the back and joined them.

Only the chickens' clucking and Dark Sunshine's lonely nickers broke the quiet.

*Perfect,* Sam thought. There'd be no noise, no interruptions. Since Popcorn was alone in the barn corral, she decided to let Mikki sit with him there.

The day's heat filled the barn, magnifying the smell of the hay packed in bales to the barn's rafters. Ribbons of light fell through the roof, turning the hay golden, then rippling down to stripe Mikki as she opened the gate into Popcorn's corral.

Sam held Mikki off a minute.

"Once you get inside, just sit," Sam said. "Remind him you're no one to be afraid of."

Mikki's condescending laugh said Sam was wrong.

"Mikki, you can't bully half a ton of horse."

"Yeah, I know."

"Why would you want to?" Sam let the question hang between them until Mikki blew out her cheeks and shook her head, then sat.

Sam stood outside the corral.

Dark Sunshine nickered from the round pen. The slats in the fence were set so close together, the mare could barely see out. She and Jake had thought that would give the mare the closed feeling she longed for. Now, the buckskin seemed to want company. Sam would have gone to her if she hadn't been put in charge of Mikki.

Sam alternated between watching Mikki and Popcorn watch each other and trying to attract Brynna's attention. Sam had slipped the bill of sale into her pocket, but she was still deciding what to do about it. She itched to know if Brynna had more information about Dark Sunshine or the rustlers before she handed it over.

But Brynna was strolling around the ranch with Dad, pointing and gesturing. Although they never got within earshot, Sam knew Brynna was making plans for the HARP program.

The more Sam thought about it, the more she liked the idea of HARP. What she didn't like was the way Dad was smiling. If he distrusted the government and blamed BLM for the high cost of grazing, why was he strolling around grinning at Brynna Olson?

Brynna might get the wrong idea.

When Gram called from the porch that dinner

was ready, Sam felt relieved. Dad would return to acting normal as soon as they sat around the kitchen table.

"Slip on out," Sam said to Mikki.

Popcorn followed the girl three steps toward the gate.

"I don't think he's mad at me," Mikki said, and her face said even more. Mikki's blue eyes danced, her mouth wore a real little-kid smile, and her cheeks flushed with satisfaction. She was actually happy.

Then something made both Mikki and Sam look across the ranch yard. Near the house, Brynna patted Dad on the back. That wouldn't have been so bad if Dad hadn't stopped and faced Brynna as if she'd meant something by it.

*What's going on?* Sam wondered. Whatever it was, it was *not* all business. Sam tried to make an excuse, but she couldn't say anything. If only Mikki hadn't noticed . . . but she had.

"Ha ha." Mikki gave a fake laugh like a donkey's bray. "You thought your dad was so perfect."

Too forcefully, Sam bolted the gate.

What did Dad's expression mean? Would Dad and Brynna start dating? Aunt Sue had gone out occasionally. Hair upswept and formal, she'd attended the symphony with men in stuffy-looking suits. But Dad and Brynna were looking at each other as if something had changed.

What if they fell in love? Would they marry and

expect her to make room for a stepmother? No. She'd only just come back home. Dad wouldn't shut her out of a decision that big.

Sam started back to the house without giving Mikki the satisfaction of a reply.

Still, Mikki kept talking. "Just watch. For the rest of the night, they'll have no time for either of us. First, they'll stare at each other with goo-goo eyes." Mikki made a sappy face to demonstrate. "Then, after dinner, they'll tell us to get lost."

Mikki sounded like a specialist on selfish adults. But the expert status didn't make her happy. Mikki's lips drooped as if her satisfied smile had never been there.

"Thanks so much for inviting us, Grace," Brynna said as the five sat down for dinner.

It took Sam a second to realize Brynna was talking to Gram. Had Brynna ever called her Grace before? Was Gram part of this romantic conspiracy?

Without thinking, Sam glanced at Mikki. She turned away when Mikki flashed a told-you-so smirk.

Though she loved tacos, Sam chewed slowly, as if the tortillas were filled with sawdust.

Conversation bumped along. Gram and Brynna did most of the talking, and Brynna claimed she had no information about Dark Sunshine or the rustlers. What she *did* say was so boring, Sam nearly dug the bill of sale out of her pocket and flaunted it.

But then she'd get in trouble, and Mikki would be delighted. If there was ever a case of misery-loves-company, Mikki was it.

In fact, Sam did everything she could to avoid meeting Mikki's gloating eyes.

She even studied Brynna. This time yesterday, Sam would have assumed Brynna was telling the truth about not knowing anything. Or, at worst, that Brynna had official government reasons for not telling all she knew.

Now, Sam figured Brynna just had a giddy crush on Dad and her high-powered brain had conked out.

Dinner ended and Sam couldn't wait for Brynna and Mikki to go, but Gram wasn't done playing hostess.

"Coffee will be ready in a few minutes," Gram said. "Sam, please set out cream and sugar."

Sam told herself she wasn't depressed. She was simply tired. After all, she'd stayed up most of the night with Dark Sunshine. Still, she felt as if she moved in slow motion, carrying the creamer and sugar bowl with underwater slowness.

Mikki looked so fascinated by the sugar cubes, Sam thought the girl might snatch one and pop it into her mouth.

"Who wants fudge cake?" Gram asked.

Sam didn't moan. She resigned herself to believing this torture would never end.

Hands went up, including Mikki's. "I do, but please, can I run out to see if Popcorn will take a sugar cube from me? I'll be back before you serve dessert. I promise."

Since Gram always thought the best of everyone, Sam looked at Dad. He was watching Brynna smile at Mikki as if she hadn't noticed the girl smirking all through dinner.

"Hurry," Brynna said. "We'll wait for you."

Sam cleared dinner plates and wondered why she was the only one who heard phoniness in Mikki's voice. She rinsed the plates at the sink and looked toward the barn. She couldn't see Mikki.

Sam took a guilty glance toward Gram. Pleased at having company, Gram hummed as she sliced extra-thick slabs of cake.

Sam scolded herself. She'd promised to give Mikki another chance, but she wasn't doing a very good job of it. She carried the cake plates to the table before Gram could ask.

Mikki returned right away, and if anyone else noticed that the girl reeked of cigarette smoke, they didn't say anything.

*Why not?* Sam knew that if Dad thought she'd smoked anywhere, let alone near the barn and horses, she'd be grounded for life.

Gram invited Brynna and Mikki to stay and watch television, or play Scrabble, but Brynna was already standing.

She looked uneasy, as if she'd just noticed Mikki's too-sweet temperament. Brynna sounded strained as she said good-bye and herded Mikki toward the door.

Dad beat her to it. With a gentlemanly bow, he opened the door, then stood there, blocking it.

He froze, hands gripping the doorframe.

"Wyatt?" Gram said. "What is it?"

Even then, Sam knew she'd never forget the awful despair in her father's voice.

"Oh, Lord, phone Luke Ely and have him call out the volunteers. The bunkhouse is on fire and the flames are reaching for the barn."

## Chapter Thirteen ❧

RIVER BEND RANCH was burning.

Dad ran and Sam followed.

Black smoke corkscrewed into the evening sky. There wasn't much smoke yet. In fact, the yard was bright as noon and popping filled the air.

Sam hesitated in the middle of the yard and stared around. On her left, the horses in the ten-acre pasture ran in a tight, nervous herd. Ahead stood the barn, full of horses and winter's hay. No smoke. No fire.

She felt relieved, then even more relieved as she saw that Dad was right—black smoke came from the old bunkhouse.

Sam took off after Dad, and her relief ended the instant she came face-to-face with a sheet of orange flame three times taller than the ruined old building it consumed.

A wall of heat stopped her.

"Hose!" Dad shouted, and Sam jumped as he

jerked the hose leading to the barn. It stretched behind him as he shot water on the blaze.

*At least the old bunkhouse is empty.* That's what Sam thought, until an arm of flame reached toward the barn and sparks peppered the air overhead.

The other hose was by the ten-acre pasture. She usually used it to fill the troughs, but would it reach this far?

"What can I do?" Brynna demanded.

Sam had left her manners in the kitchen. "Nothing," she yelled, and brushed on past.

She felt an illogical rage toward the woman. Brynna had brought Mikki here. Brynna hadn't watched her. Worse than that, Brynna had distracted Dad so that even he, so careful and slow to trust, had missed the threat in Mikki.

Only Jake had noticed. Sam missed his solid common sense. She wished he were there. But Jake was in Darton, along with Dallas and Pepper and Ross.

Saving the barn was up to her and Dad.

Sam grabbed the hose, cranked the handle on, and ran. She hit the end of the hose so hard she was nearly jerked off her feet.

The hose was way short of the old bunkhouse. The arcing stream of water barely reached the new one.

"Wet it down," Brynna said, pointing.

"Good idea," Sam admitted. If she watered the new

bunkhouse, it might not catch fire from the sparks swarming over the roof.

Even as Sam aimed for the bunkhouse roof, the water pressure lagged and fear yanked at her heart.

Dad's complaints about the well had always sounded like background noise. Now, his words made sense. Though they'd bought the new pump part, they hadn't dug the well deeper. That job cost thousands of dollars.

This wasn't like the city. Once these hoses used up all the water in the well, she and Dad would have to wait for the pump to suck up more.

They couldn't wait.

From the barn pen, Popcorn neighed nervously. Ace and Sweetheart answered from the adjoining pasture.

This smoke didn't smell like a fireplace; it was acrid and bitter. If it burned her eyes and nose, what was it doing to the animals? Sam wanted to comfort them, but she couldn't leave the hose.

Nearby, Dark Sunshine's hooves hammered in the round pen, trying to flee whatever lurked outside, frightening the other horses.

"You're all right, girl," Sam shouted, but the hooves ran on and on.

"The roof!" Suddenly Gram was beside Sam, pointing.

The old bunkhouse roof buckled into a vee and

quaked. There was a plastic smell as something inside burned hotter, then the roof collapsed and vanished.

That old roof had been built of wood. The barn roof was covered with tin. The house and new bunkhouse roofs wore some sort of shingles. Not wood. Would that make them safer?

One spark through the barn window into the hay loft could mean disaster, Sam thought, and that's when the water stopped. Sam shook the nozzle. She looked behind, but no kink in the hose had stopped the water flow.

She threw the hose aside, detoured around Brynna and Gram, who were dragging bunks, clothes, and cooking pots out of the new bunkhouse, and ran toward Dad.

He strode toward her, his face so red it looked sunburned. The fire had outlasted his attempts to quench it. Now it rose behind him in a wavering red-orange tower. Instead of crackling, the flames roared like a huge truck speeding down on them.

"What are we going to do?" Sam shouted.

"Pray for Luke to hurry." Dad stared at the front gate, as if he could will the red volunteer fire truck to appear.

Sam looked, too, but there was no truck with Luke Ely at the wheel and Jake's brothers piled in the back, and no sound of the siren that would bring neighbors to help.

Dark Sunshine began screaming. For days, the mare had pushed back her terror, trying to understand. Now the smoke and shouting and confinement freed her fear. The little buckskin whinnied for help, and Sam knew she'd lied to the horse. She'd told Dark Sunshine that she was all right, but nothing was all right.

"Make her stop!" Mikki stood on the front porch, hands pressed to her ears.

"You stupid little brat! Do you see what you did? My home is burning and it's your fault!" Sam lunged toward Mikki.

"Sam!" Dad's voice was like a slap. "Don't waste time."

Sam turned away from the crying girl. Dad was right. Nothing she did to Mikki would help.

Suddenly the siren wailed over the fire's roar. Nothing had ever sounded so good. The truck sped over the bridge and through the gate with mere inches on each side. The tires scuffed to a stop, and Jake's brothers, dressed in the yellow suspendered pants and coats called "turnouts" were everywhere. They worked levers and unrolled hose, moving with an efficiency that said they'd need every second to beat this fire.

Gram and Brynna paused by the mound they'd hauled out of the bunkhouse to watch Luke Ely jump down from the fire truck.

Luke's long jaw looked as if his teeth were set together as he approached Dad. "Where do you want to start?"

"The barn and the bunkhouse." Dad pointed index fingers in two directions.

Luke gave a quick shake of his head. "Can't do that."

"We've *got* to do that," Dad snapped. "The bunkhouse is practically new, and the barn has the winter's hay and—"

Luke clamped a hand on Dad's shoulder. The two tall men stood eye-to-eye. Dad didn't shrug off Luke's hand. He would have, if he'd been angry.

Dad was scared. The realization made Sam feel as if the earth had crumbled beneath her feet.

"Wyatt, this is just a five-hundred-gallon tanker." Luke pointed at the fire truck. "We can fight this fire for ten minutes. Fifteen, if there's a miracle."

"The Darton fire department should be here by then," Dad said.

"Maybe," Luke said. "But this is the deal right now. If you try to save them both, you're going to lose them both."

Sam's throat closed in panic, but Dad didn't falter for even a second.

"Let's get some water on that barn."

Every time the wind blew hard, Sam had heard a corner of the barn's tin roof creak, blowing up and down as the wind tried to peel it loose.

The fire found it right away. In spite of the two fire hoses, a streamer of flame swirled on the roof. It started small, but in a single minute it became a red line of fire. So straight someone might have drawn it there with a marker, the flame licked down the corner of the barn.

Although they'd given the old bunkhouse up as a lost cause, the fire thrived there, creating its own whirring wind. All at once, the wind shifted.

Sparks hit the ten-acre pasture, and Sam heard Buddy cry. When Buddy bucked and bawled, Sam knew the calf had been singed. Luke and Dad shouted over the fire's roar. Sam ran closer to hear what they were saying, in time to hear one of Jake's brothers curse at a hose.

Water from Luke Ely's hose kept coming, but it flowed in pulses. It wouldn't last.

Sam looked at her watch. The fire truck had been there for ten minutes, but there was no sign of the big tanker from Darton. Every horse on the ranch was screaming as the ten-acre pasture began to burn. Dad shot one last, demanding look toward the gate, then turned to Sam.

"We've got to set the horses loose. Seth"—Dad pointed at the closest Ely brother—"unlatch these two corrals." Dad gestured toward the ten-acre pasture, but Gram was already waving her arm in the air, signaling she knew what to do.

Dad turned to Sam. "Sam, get on Ace and make

sure the horses get through the gate. When the truck comes from Darton, we don't want a bunch of crazed horses milling around, getting in the way. Forget the saddle," he shouted.

Sam shook her head. What had she been thinking? She'd actually started toward the barn, headed for the tack room to get Ace's saddle and bridle. Instead, she unsnapped a lead rope draped over a fence. Out in the barn pasture, Ace wore a halter. That would have to be enough.

"Sam, can you do this?" Dad was already looking over the Ely boys, ready to choose one to take her place.

Sam took a deep breath, and it hurt.

"I can do it," she insisted, then scrambled over the fence before she could change her mind.

Ace trotted toward her, head tossing so that his black forelock flew away from his white star. He didn't care if she carried a halter rope. He wanted the reassurance a human could bring.

The grass brushed damp around her ankles, and Sam told herself she was foolish to worry. She had ridden bareback all during her childhood. One terrible accident hadn't robbed her of all her skills. She could do this.

Ace ducked his head. She snapped on the lead and flung herself toward his back. She scrambled up, closed her legs around Ace's warm body, and headed him toward the pasture gate Seth Ely had swung open.

Sweetheart bolted past, her pinto body bright in the firelight. Ace jogged through the gate, head pulling left, then right, snorting and grunting. Then Popcorn joined Sweetheart, and the ranch yard was filled with horses.

Gram and Brynna waved their arms, trying to haze the horses toward the gate. Banjo took the lead. The bald-faced bay ran with his mouth open, body lean and lowered to the ground. He headed for open range. The others galloped after him.

Sam had decided it was time to free Ace, too, when a pale shape separated from the bunch of saddle horses. Popcorn was doubling back.

The confused mustang ran a zigzag path, returning to the barn pen. And the fire.

"No!" Sam shouted.

Ace whirled on his haunches, cutting Popcorn off as if he'd been a rebellious cow.

For a minute they were so close together that Sam saw the puzzlement in Popcorn's crystal-blue eyes. First Mikki's panicky punishment, now the fire. Poor Popcorn. How could he trust when things kept going so wrong?

Even with Ace pushing against him, Popcorn tried to shove past, toward the fire.

"No!" Sam shouted again, but this time she spun

the end of the halter rope, shooing him back.

It worked. In two long leaps, Popcorn joined the other horses. In another leap, he'd caught Banjo. Sam kept Ace at a lope, but as soon as all of the horses were out of the ranch yard, running toward the open range, she pulled him to a stop.

Ace danced in place, head tossing, barely under control. Smoke and dust whirled around them as Sam slipped off and planted her feet. She tugged on the halter rope, but Ace didn't settle down. With short, fearful neighs, he bumped her. Sam fumbled with the snap on the halter rope. Her hands were shaking, and though affection kept Ace from knocking her flat on purpose, he would, sooner or later.

*There*. The gelding felt his freedom. He wheeled away from her, following the other horses.

Sam didn't watch them run away. She glanced down the dark and empty road, then turned toward the ranch yard, toward the fire. She jogged, though her smoke-tortured lungs protested.

*Please don't let it take the barn. Please save the house.* Sam didn't know if she muttered the words or just thought them, but her pleas were interrupted by shrill cries.

Dark Sunshine. No one had freed the mare. The round pen shuddered from the impact of her body as she tried to batter her way out.

Panting, wondering where everyone else had

gone, Sam slid the latch free. Before she could open the gate, the buckskin mare exploded through. Once in the open yard, she stood amazed and disoriented.

"That way!" Sam shouted, and ran at the mare. The horse jumped back, and Sam felt an instant's regret that last night's gentling had been wasted. Then her eyes fell on her own shadow, cast black and perfect by the fire behind her.

"Go!" she yelled, whirling the rope.

The mare ran, and Sam pursued her all the way to the gate.

Only then did she hear the sirens. The Darton fire department, all three trucks, huffed down the road toward the River Bend entrance.

The first truck had already turned, maneuvering its huge bulk through the gate, when Dark Sunshine reached it.

Horror and smoke snatched Sam's breath. She couldn't get even a sip of oxygen. They were going to collide. The delicate buckskin mare was no match for tons of steel and iron.

Dark Sunshine leaped over the cattle guard, inches ahead of the truck's bumper. She galloped on, turned golden by the next set of headlights, then swerved so quickly she seemed to have been brushed aside by a giant hand.

Even as the trucks passed her, Sam watched the mare. She was running wild now, catching Ross's big horse, Tank, at the back of the herd, passing Sweetheart, then Strawberry, Ace, and even Popcorn.

Dark Sunshine was racing for the lead, and Sam was sure she'd never come back.

## Chapter Fourteen ❧

ꟻIRE HOSES CRISSCROSSED the ranch yard. A young woman wearing head-to-toe firefighter gear paused, flipped up the visor on her helmet, and smiled at Sam.

"We'll have this knocked down in a couple of minutes," she said, jerking a thumb toward the barn. "No problem."

"Thanks," Sam mumbled, but the woman had already jogged on to join the others.

They turned on floodlights and worked together as a team. Sam didn't look away until Buddy's head butted into her palm and stayed there.

"Why didn't you go with the horses, Buddy?" Sam knelt in front of the calf and hugged her neck. "You silly baby."

As Sam's hands moved over the calf's body, she felt a few crispy places and smelled the acrid scent of burned hair, but Buddy didn't flinch.

The calf settled beside Sam on the front porch.

Together, they watched the flames shrink and the smoke turn white. The firefighters kept watering the barn and old bunkhouse, but their movements had turned from urgent to leisurely. The volunteers were packing to go home.

The horses had escaped, and though they might be tough to regather, they were safe. Dad coughed as he helped the Elys roll up the hose, but he hadn't been burned. Gram looked fine, too.

In fact, she moved like a teenager, lean and quick in her jeans as she walked Brynna and Mikki back to the BLM truck. The car door slammed, sealing Mikki safely inside. Brynna stood waving as Gram walked away.

This night could have been a lot worse, Sam mused.

Somehow she missed the arrival of Jake and his mom until Jake's shadow fell over her. Sam looked up at his broad shoulders and tipped-down Stetson, and she gave a tired smile.

"How ya doin', Brat?" His voice rumbled with something like concern, and Sam jumped up to hug him. "I wish—I *would've* been here, but I went to a movie with my mom." He talked over Sam's shoulder, since she refused to budge. "She likes that mother-son stuff 'cause I'm her baby, y'know?"

Sam nodded but didn't speak. Jake was no baby. He felt solid and dependable, and he was her best friend. She gave him one last squeeze, then stepped back.

She almost laughed when she noticed Jake rubbing

the back of his neck. When Dad used that gesture, it meant he was thinking or embarrassed. Right now, Sam would bet on the latter.

"Must've, uh, been a pretty bad night," Jake managed.

Sam sniffed, feeling a little sheepish.

"Don't let a little hug go to your head," Sam said. "I just hugged Buddy, too."

Jake's answer was half laugh, half groan, and Sam enjoyed his confusion until her eyes caught movement across the yard.

"I guess hugging is contagious." Sam's lips felt cold. She barely got the words out as she stared.

Jake looked over his shoulder. "Yeah, my mom's like that after a fire. She thinks Dad should stick to ranching. She says that's dangerous enough."

Sam glanced at Jake's parents, hugging beside the volunteer fire truck. She sighed. "I wasn't looking at them."

"Honest?" Jake looked around the yard.

Sam could tell when Jake saw what she did. He froze.

Dad was doing more than hugging Brynna Olson. He was kissing her.

Sam's hand went to her pocket. The bill of sale still crinkled inside. She knew how to get Brynna away from her father.

"Could you watch Buddy for a minute?" she asked Jake.

"I'll put her back in the pasture. She'll be lonely, but no fire truck will back over her."

"Thanks," she said. Sam felt like she was striding through a cold and narrow tunnel as she headed across the yard. She ignored Dad's embarrassment and faced Brynna.

The redhead's expression was so understanding, Sam wanted to scream. *Save your sympathy*, she wanted to say. *I can take care of myself.* But she didn't scream, only shoved the piece of yellow paper toward Brynna's hand.

"I think you'll want to look at this," she said.

"Sam, what is it?"

"Just look at it," Sam said.

She watched Brynna's expression turn professional, as if nothing had happened. Suddenly she couldn't stand watching them together for another second. She darted across the yard past Jake and into the house.

Once inside, she took the stairs two at a time, then growled with frustration when she cranked on the shower only to have water dribble out in teaspoons.

Sam returned to her room and buried her face in her hands. She *really* needed a shower. She smelled awful. The odor was more like toxic waste than wood smoke. She was polluting her own bedroom. She looked at Jingles, perched on her pillow, and nearly apologized.

"And I know they'll make me go to school tomorrow," she moaned to the plush horse. "Who cares if my house almost burned down, my horse is gone, Dark Sunshine belongs to a criminal, and my father has chosen this as a great time to get a crush on Brynna Olson?"

Gram had loved Louise, her mother. Maybe Gram could talk some sense into Dad.

Sam set her alarm clock for five-thirty instead of six. It would take her that long to scrub the stink from her hair and skin.

She plopped into bed. She resolved to stay awake and talk to Gram when she came up, but she never heard a thing.

The next day turned out to be Sunday.

When Sam ran downstairs freshly showered and hungry for breakfast, she was alone. It took her only a few minutes to realize her mistake, but she decided not to waste her early start.

Since she couldn't go ride, Sam made herself toast and jam and sat at the kitchen table reading a story she'd been assigned for English class.

It was really a pretty good story. Sam was stretching and smiling, thinking she could spend more time on homework now that Mikki wouldn't be coming over. Certainly, HARP would get rid of a kid that destructive.

Sam was pouring herself more juice when she heard something hit the front porch. *Weird*, she thought as the heavy thing struck again.

When the sound continued and Blaze began barking, curiosity pulled Sam to the kitchen window. A horse stood with his front hooves on the porch. One of those hooves pawed at the porch for attention.

"Ace!" Sam burst through the door and let it slam.

Her horse was dusty. Clumps of burrs studded his tail, and his deep neigh probably wasn't a greeting but a demand for breakfast. Still, he was home.

Sweetheart had come back with him. She circled, tossing her head for attention, near the ten-acre pasture where Dallas, Ross, and Pepper were just crawling out of sleeping bags.

Sam could imagine how smokey and unpleasant it had been inside the bunkhouse, and she couldn't blame them for sleeping outside.

She had fed and brushed both horses, checked out the fire and water damage to the barn, and searched—unsuccessfully—for the hens when Jake and Jen rode into the yard.

Sam's heart swelled at the sight of her friends. Jake sat loosely in the saddle on Witch and Jen rode her palomino. Because she'd brought another horse for Sam to ride, Sam knew they'd come to help search for the scattered horses.

"I didn't think your horses would be back," Jen started.

"They're not—just Ace and Sweetheart, and they look like they've been running half the night."

"It's a good thing I brought Kitty, then," Jen said. "She's not as skittish as she looks."

Jen held up reins leading to an alert sorrel whose nostrils worked constantly as she took in the smells of smoke and charred wood.

"You guys are great." Sam smiled at Jake and walked toward Jen. She stroked the shoulder of the wary sorrel. "And Kitty, pretty Kitty, can act however she likes, because she's my Blackie's mom."

"You make her behave once you mount up," Jake ordered.

Sam started to ask Jake who the heck he thought he was, but the worry lines around his eyes stopped her.

"Thanks, Jen," she said. "I'd like to give Ace a rest."

By mid-afternoon, all the horses except Dark Sunshine were headed for home.

Once the three friends got them past the road to the BLM corrals and the pond at War Drum Flats, the horses broke into a rolling lope toward River Bend Ranch.

All except Popcorn. River Bend hadn't been his home for long, and the albino was so jumpy they'd had to herd him most of the way. Now, within sight of the ranch, he seemed to remember the shelter and grain, and trotted along without being pushed.

*If only Dark Sunshine was trotting beside him*, Sam

thought. Jen must have understood her sigh.

"I bet the buckskin's joined up with a wild herd," Jen said. Their horses fell back to a walk, with Sam riding in the middle.

Sam imagined the Phantom rounding the mare up and adding her to his harem. She'd be so much happier, knee-deep in grass in a wild horse canyon, with soaring red rock walls to hide her from cruel men.

Sam's mind wandered from that happy image, to the bill of sale, to the revelation Dad had made just a few nights ago.

"Oh, my gosh," Sam gasped. "What does the government do to you if you lose a foster horse and it's a horse that maybe shouldn't have been fostered by the BLM in the first place?"

Jen cocked her head to one side, thinking, and a white-blond braid swung free. "Give me a minute to unravel that one," she said, frowning.

Jake wasn't half as sympathetic.

"Why do I get the feeling," he said, eyes fixed forward as he trotted beside Sam, "that this is the start of something I don't want to hear?"

"Is this about the B.O.S.?" Jen asked cryptically.

*Bill of sale*. Sam nodded.

"It is," Sam said, ignoring Jake's irritation. "And it's not really a secret anymore."

"What do you mean?" Jen looked rather sickly. Sam couldn't blame her for not wanting to be implicated in a federal crime.

"The cat's out of the bag," Sam said. "I decided to give the bill of sale to Brynna."

"Bill of sale for what?" Jake demanded.

"I told you not to tell him." Jen's singsong voice made Jake shoot her a glare.

"For Dark Sunshine," Sam mumbled, but there was no doubt Jake heard.

"Where did you get a bill of sale for—" Jake broke off. "If you were tampering with a crime scene—" He stopped and glanced from Sam to Jen, then back to Sam. "I *know* you weren't doing that. Even a couple of featherbrains like you two would know better than—"

Jen leaned forward in her saddle, arguing past Sam.

"That's just where we found it, Jake Ely. Right where you and those federal officers couldn't." Jen gathered her reins and eased her palomino into a fluid lope.

Sam turned toward Jake. A dozen sarcastic responses showed in his expression, but he didn't allow even one to escape. Good. Maybe if he was finished bickering with Jen, he could help figure things out.

Instead, Jake spoke very patiently.

"Are you saying," Jake began, "that you let Brynna award you foster care of that mare when you knew she belonged to someone else, and you even knew who?"

"Of course not," Sam said. "We didn't find the bill

of sale until two days afterward."

"So, who does she belong to?"

"Curtis . . ." Sam began, but she couldn't remember the rest.

"Flickinger," Jen supplied.

Jake's lower lip poked out a little as he considered the name. "Not from around here," he said. "But maybe Brynna can put him in some government database and see what she comes up with."

"Except he *didn't* adopt the horse," Sam said. "He bought her from Rose Bloom, the lady who adopted Dark Sunshine just over a year ago and got title to her." Sam paused for a breath. "So she could legally sell her to this guy."

"Curtis Flickinger," Jen repeated, slowly. She wet her lips, glanced back toward the pond with a considering look, then shook her head. "Sam? I—wow, I almost know that name."

"Wishful thinking," Jake dismissed her. "Didn't Brynna say the horse was from out of state?"

"Captured in Oregon and taken to Idaho, then Wyoming," Sam admitted.

Jake leaned forward again, and flashed Jen a satisfied look.

But Jen wouldn't be silenced. "Yeah, like cowboys don't move around a lot."

"Who said the guy was a cowboy?" Jake snapped back. "Because he's a rustler, he has to be a cowboy?"

Sam hated being in the middle. This had to stop.

"You know what's wrong with you two?" Sam interrupted. Jen and Jake glared at her. "You both have to be right."

Jen shrugged. They rode in silence for a minute.

"I'm headed for home," Jake said, as if Sam hadn't said a thing. "I need to get Witch rubbed down, then help my dad with some fool thing he said he'd do for Slocum's party."

"Brahma-que," Jen corrected.

"Yeah, well, just shoot me if I say that in public," Jake answered. Then he reined his black mare away from them and jogged toward home.

"Give me a minute, Sam," Jen said. "I'll remember where I've heard that name."

Kitty saw the white BLM truck first.

Sam had been surprised at how well she and the sorrel had been getting on, but now Kitty shied and threatened to bolt. Sam regained control in just a minute, but it was clear the truck had frightened the mare.

Sam leaned forward, petting Kitty's neck. "It's okay, girl. I'm getting pretty darn sick of seeing that truck myself."

"I don't know what you two are mumbling about, but Miss Olson's slowing down," Jen said.

Sam glanced back. If Brynna wanted to apologize for Mikki, she could save her breath. And if she wanted to talk about kissing Dad . . . she'd better keep driving.

Brynna stopped. As she lowered her truck window, Jen gasped.

"BLM," she said. "That's it." Wide-eyed, she looked at Sam. "Flickinger. Flick. Remember?"

Sam felt her brain trying to catch up. She was almost there when Jen blurted her conclusion to Brynna.

"It's him, isn't it?" Jen asked. "Curtis Flickinger is Flick, that guy with the long droopy mustache who used to work for Slocum."

Brynna nodded. "I checked BLM's payroll records and it is him. He worked for us while he was working for Slocum," she said.

Brynna stared at Sam. Then, just in case Sam had forgotten one of the worst days of her life, Brynna added, "Curtis Flickinger is the man who caught the Phantom."

## Chapter Fifteen ❧

SAM GRABBED THE saddle horn.

On the cattle drive, Flick had made her miserable. It had been her first week back in Nevada, and he'd mocked her horsemanship and called her a dude. He'd teased Jake, saying he'd better take care of his "little girlfriend." Flick also made a point of calling mustangs "range rats."

She might have forgiven it as "joshing" if he hadn't captured the Phantom.

Flick was an incredible roper, on horseback or afoot. Yards of lariat flew and tightened at his whim. That's why Slocum had hired him to rope the Phantom.

"It *was* Flick up there," Sam realized. "He'd shaved off his mustache, but . . ." Sam saw the scene at Lost Canyon replaying in her mind. "It was his lazy way of tossing his loop, and he used the whip the same way. It's him."

In Lost Canyon, Flick had missed his throw for the Phantom. Instead of feeling hopeful, despair weighed Sam down. Flick was too good to miss a second time.

"Law enforcement has done casts of the tire tread from the truck and trailer in Lost Canyon," Brynna said. "But they won't do us much good until we have a real tire to compare with them."

"So you'd have to impound a truck, then, see if they match, right?" Jen asked.

Brynna nodded. "I have a theory, which might hurry things up a little."

Jen leaned forward in her saddle, listening. Sam was interested, but she straightened an edge of saddle blanket instead of looking into Brynna's eyes.

"If they branded those horses the day they trapped them, the burns shouldn't look fresh by now. Add that to the fact they've had time to fatten them up, and I think the rustlers will bring them to the Mineral auction yards this Tuesday."

"And you're going to be waiting for them," Jen said.

"Right, with a brand inspector and two rangers. But it would help if I had a witness to verify they're the right guys."

Sam couldn't help but look up then. She was the only witness.

"On Tuesday?" Sam asked.

"If I get Wyatt's permission for you to miss

school, would you ride along with me?"

Brynna's expression was hopeful. Sam knew there was more at stake here than the rustlers. Brynna wanted Sam to like her, to approve of her affection for Dad.

Sam didn't want to go, but how could she refuse? The rustlers were a danger to all horses. The Phantom, his herd, maybe Dark Sunshine, could be trapped and sold for dog meat.

"Okay," Sam said, but she looked away from Brynna's smile.

That night, Sam sat up late.

She'd finished her homework and slipped it inside her backpack. She'd put out clothes for the morning and was about to throw her dirty jeans in with the laundry when she remembered the hair from the Phantom's mane, stuffed in her pocket.

Sam ran her fingers through the silky, silvery strands. She'd hoped they'd send a message to Dark Sunshine, and now it was too late. Just the same, she wove the hair into a tiny braid. *Let Zanzibar stay safe.* Sam lifted the right strands over the middle ones. *Let Dark Sunshine stop being terrified.* If the men who'd abused the buckskin caught her again, what would become of the mare?

Sam lifted the left strands and braided them in.

Hope was plaited with every strand, but hope wasn't enough. As Sam knotted the ends and slid the bracelet over her wrist, she vowed to be brave. She had not done enough to help catch those rustlers, but that was about to change.

Sam ambushed Jake in Darton High's rally court, a grassy rectangle in the center of the school and a busy place during lunch.

"I'll be right back," she told Jen.

"Don't take no for an answer," Jen said. "Next time it could be Silly or Ace."

Sam nodded and gave Jen a thumbs-up. Then, working like a cow pony, Sam cut Jake out from the rest of his friends.

A few of the guys made comments, and Darrell, with his baggy pants and lazy-lidded eyes, gave Sam an approving nod as she towed Jake away.

"What is it?" Jake crossed his arms and waited.

"If those rustlers don't show up at the auction tomorrow, you have to help me catch them. And you can just quit looking like I've gone nuts, Jake Ely, because those rustlers *will* be hiding from the rangers. We could go up the canyon during Slocum's Brahma-que, when no one else is out driving around. We can catch them, I know it. They won't suspect a couple of teenagers."

"There's a good reason for that, Sam."

Sam stared at him. Jen had convinced her silence could be an effective argument. She waited.

"Why me?" Jake complained. "Why don't you get Jen—"

Jake must have seen her satisfaction, because he shut his jaw and glanced over to where Jen waited.

"What am I saying? You and Jen riding alone in the canyon? They're criminals. There's no telling what they'd do. I won't be part of this."

"That's too bad." Sam shrugged. "I could've used your help."

"I'm telling Wyatt."

"Do you know how immature that sounds?" Sam wanted to wipe the smile from Jake's lips. He thought he had her now. "You were never a tattletale, Jake."

He stayed quiet. How could she have thought she'd win the silence game over Jake?

"What if they'd rounded up our horses while they were loose? What would you have told Mr. Martinez if they'd gotten Teddy Bear?"

Jake's eyes opened a millimeter wider, encouraging Sam to keep talking.

"I need you to do this with me," she insisted, "because you're really good at tracking, because you can drive"—Sam dashed her fingers through her auburn bangs—"and because I'm a little afraid to do it alone."

"You should be, Brat. It's dangerous."

Frustrated, Sam looked past Jake to where his

friends stood waiting. Darrell was using the time to slick back his hair. Sam thought about saying *I bet he'd help me*, but she didn't. Instead, she told Jake the one thing he didn't know about the rustlers.

"The rustler in the gray hat who acted like a cowboy, who tried to rope the Phantom? He's Flick."

Jake's face grew still. She'd heard Flick harass Jake and seen the unspoken scorn that had to do with Jake being Shoshone. What other grudges might Jake have against Flick?

The bell rang, ending the lunch hour.

"I'll think about it," he mumbled, and moved back toward his friends.

Gram and Sam drove into the ranch yard after school to find Mikki sitting on the front porch, alone.

"What is she doing here?"

"I'm rather surprised myself," Gram said.

"Jake's not here," Sam said. "What should I do?"

"Let her work with a horse, I'd say." Gram climbed from the car and Sam had no chance to argue.

As Sam faced Mikki, she could smell the charred wood soaked by fire hoses. The stench still hung over the ranch yard, following Sam as she passed the blackened posts, all that remained of the old bunkhouse.

For once, Mikki looked her age. She wore a wrinkled yellow tee shirt and jeans. Her knees were tucked up against her chest with her arms wrapped around them. Instead of being moussed into spikes, her hair lay close to her head. She looked like a dejected baby duck.

Sam did not feel sorry for Mikki. The girl had traumatized Popcorn. She'd set the ranch on fire. She'd gloated over Dad liking Brynna. Sam stood next to Mikki and looked down on her.

"If Brynna reports me, I'm out of the HARP program for good."

*If?* Sam couldn't believe there was any doubt.

"Do you think she will?" Sam asked.

"Why wouldn't she?" Mikki snapped, but then she seemed to melt. "After I did this pilot program, I was supposed to be able to come back in the summer. And if I did really good, Brynna said I might be able to assist in one of the California programs. I'd be working with horses all the time, if I didn't get in any trouble." Mikki's voice soared, then stopped.

Chin in her hands, Mikki stared out at the ten-acre pasture. Buddy was touching noses with Teddy Bear. Strawberry and Banjo stood head-to-tail, swishing the flies from each other's faces.

If Mikki didn't get in trouble with HARP, she would with Dad. Sam knew that for sure.

"You'll know soon enough," Sam said. "So, you'd better take advantage of today." She reached for Mikki's wrist and tugged the girl to her feet. "Popcorn was doing all right before." Sam didn't slow down when Mikki faltered.

"He was just watching me, is all."

"Watching, but then he followed you a few steps as you left, remember? We put him in the round pen since . . ." Sam swallowed. "Since Dark Sunshine is still gone."

"I'm sorry," Mikki said.

"You should be," Sam said. "If we do catch her, she could be hurt, or crazy." Sam stopped and reined in her anger.

Before she unlatched the gate to the round pen, Popcorn's nicker greeted them. "Go on in. I'll bring you a scoop of grain. He might be ready to eat from your hand."

"If he does, will you tell Brynna? Maybe, if she hasn't already told, she'll know I'm good at this." Mikki looked up at Sam. "I *am*, aren't I? I just messed it up, like I always do."

*Like I always do.* Sam knew there was something important in those words. For some weird reason, Mikki wouldn't let herself succeed. But telling her that might only make it worse.

"I'm going to let you borrow something," Sam said. With careful fingers, she lifted the horsehair bracelet at her wrist and slid it off her hand. "It's made from the Phantom's mane."

Mikki stared at the bracelet as if she expected jolts of magic powers to come crackling from it.

"I might break it," she said.

"You won't."

A dozen questions chased across Mikki's face as she looked at Sam, but she didn't ask even one, just extended her bony arm.

"I'll want it back when you come out," Sam said gruffly. Because Mikki's hand was shaking so hard, Sam had to steady it to slip the bracelet on.

"I'll give it right back." Mikki nodded furiously, squared her shoulders, and walked into the pen.

Twenty minutes later, Sam peered through the close-set fence rails. It was like watching a big-screen TV. Popcorn and Mikki were right in front of her, framed by wood.

Sam saw the minute Popcorn decided he'd been lonely long enough. She saw him walk across the pen, long mane sweeping forward at each step. She saw him stop, blow through his lips, and start lipping grain from Mikki's palm.

Mikki stood statue-still. Only her braceleted arm moved from the albino's questing nose. Soon, Mikki's cheeks were shiny from tears.

When the grain was gone, the horse still stood there. Mikki's eyes slid toward the rails where Sam stood. She fixed Sam with a what-should-I-do-next? look.

The white gelding had chosen to trust Mikki, but his faith must keep building.

"Just stay there," Sam said.

Popcorn's ears pricked toward Sam's voice. His muscles rolled, ready to run if anything frightened him.

But nothing did, and Popcorn leaned forward, his muzzle thrusting at Mikki's empty hand. The girl's fingers opened. She turned her hand and gently touched the gelding's face.

Popcorn snorted. His head swung away, but his hooves stayed in place. He shifted his weight until his shoulder grazed hers. And then he leaned against Mikki as if she were another horse.

They stood that way for minutes before Sam saw Mikki's chest moving in gasps. She was trying not to scare the horse with sobs she could barely keep inside.

After a while, she made for the gate, sobs breaking as she returned the bracelet.

"I don't deserve him," Mikki managed.

"No one does," Sam said. She kept her voice low, and Popcorn didn't seem to mind. His white eyelashes fluttered as his eyes closed. "All day long we go to school and forget about horses. Then we come home and expect them to do whatever we want. And usually they do."

"But I—" Mikki's voice caught, and Popcorn's eyes opened. The girl slowed her breathing before she went on. "I didn't ignore him. I was mean to him."

Sam felt almost dizzy with responsibility. She concentrated, trying to think of a way to respond to

Mikki's confusion. Outside the ranch yard, across the bridge, La Charla rushed along. Sam heard no answers, but Mikki was waiting.

"That's how love is, I guess," Sam said. "Sometimes you get it even when you don't deserve it. All you can do is try."

Mikki's deep sigh said she was satisfied, but Sam didn't know where the words had come from.

She had the weirdest feeling that someone wise and understanding had stood beside her, telling her what to say. She'd never admit it to anyone, because it sounded crazy, but Sam could almost imagine the silent voice had been her mother's.

## Chapter Sixteen ❧

$S$AM GOT UP AT HER regular time, had cereal and toast while Gram and Dad ate omelets, and reviewed what the three rustlers looked like. If she didn't recognize them, no one would.

"I don't have to worry about identifying Flick," she told Gram and Dad. "Even without a mustache, I'll know him."

"So will Brynna." Dad's eyes didn't lift from his newspaper. "You know, it's a darn shame that woman works for the government." Quickly, Dad forked another bite in his mouth, almost as if he wanted an excuse not to explain.

Sam stared across the table at Gram, who'd paused with a coffee cup halfway to her lips. Why didn't she say something?

Gram shrugged, then coaxed Sam to keep thinking. "What about the other rustlers?"

"The one wearing camouflage was stocky, with a

broad face and freckles," Sam said. "The other one had bushy white hair and eyes like a scared rabbit."

"I don't think they're from around here," Gram said.

Neither did Sam. What if they'd taken the horses elsewhere? Brynna was probably dragging her off on a wild-goose chase.

Dad pushed his chair back from the table. He was frowning, and Sam crossed her fingers, hoping he'd come to his senses about Brynna.

"Don't plan on using Mikki with Popcorn," he said instead.

"What's going to happen?" Sam asked.

"When you get home this afternoon, there'll be a Dumpster sitting next to what's left of the bunkhouse. And Mikki will be shoveling every bit of burned wood and ash into it."

"Wyatt, that's a huge job," Gram said.

"You bet it is," he agreed. "And with every shovelful, she can look at our house and barn and the other bunkhouse and think what could've happened from her carelessness."

"What about Popcorn?" Sam asked.

"He'll keep," Dad said. "Mikki starts today. When she's finished, then we'll see about horses."

Frost clung to the edges of Brynna's windshield when she picked Sam up. She drove a tan sedan instead of her usual BLM truck, but she had on her khaki uniform and her hair was in a tight French braid. Although Brynna smiled as Sam climbed into the warm car, everything about her said "On duty."

Sam was glad. It probably meant Brynna wasn't planning on a heart-to-heart talk.

Now, Sam and Brynna were driving away from the bus stop, away from school, toward the Mineral auction yards.

Red rock formations jutted from the land around them. The last time Sam had traveled this highway, she'd been coming from the airport in Reno. Dad had been driving her toward home when they saw a BLM helicopter pursuing wild horses.

Sam smiled, remembering how she'd thought her imagination conjured up a silver stallion standing under a stone overhang. Now, she knew he'd been more than imagination.

"There he is." Brynna nodded down the road.

Sam caught her breath and stared, but Brynna wasn't pointing out the Phantom. She was looking a mile down the road as she lifted the handset of the car's police radio. Then she spoke into it.

"Hey, Jim," she said.

"Gotcha in my rearview mirror." A male voice came from the radio as a Jeep with a roof bar of amber, blue, and red lights pulled from the roadside and eased into the lane in front of them.

"That's the brand inspector, Jim McDonald," Brynna explained. "He'd be going out to Mineral anyway, but we're traveling together, just in case."

"You have Wyatt's girl with you?" asked Jim McDonald.

"I do."

"Samantha, just speak up if you see something you don't like. Or if you recognize a driver, a car, a truck—anything."

The radio voice clicked off before Sam could say she would. As they drove in silence, Brynna sipped from a Styrofoam cup of coffee.

Brynna and Jim McDonald stayed in the slow lane, so other traffic passed on the left, where Sam could peer past Brynna and take a good look.

Two cattle trucks chugged by, but Hereford steers were visible inside them both. A silver car towed a matching horse trailer past, but the paint horse inside was not one of the mustangs.

"Did Wyatt mention we were going to Slocum's Brahma-que together?" Brynna sounded nervous.

"Like a date?" Sam asked, but Brynna didn't really answer.

"He was supposed to." Brynna hit the steering wheel with the flat of her hand, which probably meant it wasn't just a car pool.

Sam twisted toward the front so quickly, the shoulder harness of her seat belt tightened.

It was bad enough Dad wanted to go out with Brynna Olson. Why couldn't he have explained it himself? Had he been about to, this morning, when he'd said he wished Brynna didn't work for the government?

Sam would bet she was the last to know. It wasn't fair.

And then Sam heard pinging. The rustler's truck had a pinging engine. She stared past Brynna to the fast lane.

The Ford truck was black, not yellow-brown like the one from Lost Canyon, but it *was* towing a stock trailer. The trailer had been painted black to match the truck, but it had an orange reflective stripe. That and the pinging convinced Sam.

"Sam, what is it?" Brynna asked.

"I think . . ." Sam shook her head. She'd feel dumb if they pulled the vehicle over and it was filled with potted plants or something. "Do you think they could have painted the truck?"

"Of course. That black Ford?" Brynna had already spotted it. She increased her speed and lifted the radio microphone. She turned to Sam once more before calling Jim McDonald. "Take a good look, Sam. Is that it?"

"Don't call," Sam fretted. "I'm not sure."

But then the truck drew ahead and she saw into the trailer. Three horses' rumps were visible: a bay, a roan, and a gleaming black.

"Do it," Sam said. "I'm almost positive it's them."

The instant Brynna spoke, the lightbar on Jim McDonald's car flashed on. Red lights bounced from one side of the bar to the other, and a siren yipped.

The black truck and trailer swayed toward the roadside, then slowed with a crunch of gravel.

Jim McDonald's car nosed in behind the trailer. Brynna stopped just inches behind him. As the brand inspector climbed out of his truck, Sam noticed he wore a gun.

Brynna switched off the car. "Let's go."

Brynna tugged on a khaki cap that matched her uniform. The pretty woman with a crush on Dad had disappeared. In her place stood a cold-eyed professional. Those rustlers had better watch out.

Jim McDonald approached on the driver's side, while Brynna strode toward the truck's passenger door.

"Stay behind the trailer," Brynna said without looking at Sam. And she did.

Gunplay in the movies was exciting, but here on a lonely Nevada road, it sounded scary.

Sam felt safer back there with the horses. As the animals jostled against each other, Sam felt certain they were the mustangs. Each wore a different brand, but even to her beginner's eye, the burns appeared to be at the same stage of healing.

The black mustang's coat was stiff with sweat. He was curious, trying to look at Sam, but each time he tried to sling his head around, he hit the side of the trailer.

Quietly, Sam smooched at him. "Okay, pretty horse. Things will get better real soon."

At the sound of Sam's voice, the roan tried to get away, but he could go nowhere. Sam stayed silent, then, afraid the animals would hurt themselves.

"Out of the truck, gentlemen." Jim McDonald sounded casual.

"What's wrong?" The voice rasped. Sam thought the voice might belong to the white-haired rustler with the bulgy eyes.

"Why'd you stop us?" said a second voice. "We ain't breakin' the speed limit."

That one sounded too young to belong to the rustlers she'd seen. What if she *had* made a mistake?

"I'm wondering if you've got some papers on these horses," Jim McDonald said, "and hoping you can show them to me."

"Why would we want to do that?" the rusty voice demanded.

"Because he's the state brand inspector," Brynna said cheerfully. "Not only can he impound this truck and trailer, he can put you two in jail if he doesn't like the look of the brands on your horses. They are branded, I suppose?"

"'Course," said the young voice.

Sam heard Jim McDonald shuffle through papers. Dissatisfied, he asked the men to unload the horses.

Truck doors creaked open, boots hit the pavement, doors slammed. Sam saw the white-haired man first. He really did have the eyes of a startled rabbit.

The other one was a gangly guy with a long chin. He wore sneakers and couldn't be over nineteen years old. Neither he nor Rabbit Eyes were eager to unload the horses. The men made aimless motions, each hoping the other would do it. Finally, Rabbit Eyes stepped forward and glared at Sam.

"Out of the way, girly."

*Girly?* Surprise kept Sam quiet until she thought of a good way to let Rabbit Eyes know that she didn't like being called *girly*. She looked past the men to Brynna and gave a firm nod.

Jim McDonald saw, but he didn't say anything right away.

The roan launched a two-hooved kick at the trailer door and the white-haired man jumped back.

"You sure this is necessary?" Rabbit Eyes asked.

"You mean to tell me you can't handle your own stock?" Jim McDonald looked startled.

"Shoot, these nags are wild as bobcats. They just came off the range."

"Which range would that be?" Brynna asked.

The rustlers looked at each other. Neither had an answer. If they named a local ranch, their story could be checked. If they said the horses had been free on BLM land, they'd be fined. They didn't know how to stay out of bigger trouble than they were already in.

"Gentlemen, I'll tell you what," said Jim McDonald. "Those documents are forged, and the way you're so afraid of 'em, I'm thinking those horses just don't belong to you."

Neither man spoke. To Sam, their silence proved the brand inspector was right.

"I'm impounding your whole rig," Jim McDonald continued. "A couple of rangers are on their way. One'll give you a ride back to the Darton jail. The other will drive these ponies to the Willow Springs holding pens until we determine who owns them."

"But they're not stolen!" the younger man shouted.

"You shut up," Rabbit Eyes grumbled.

Sam watched as Brynna and Jim zeroed in on the younger one. Even Sam saw he wasn't as committed to the crime as the older man.

"Lucky it's not the old days," Jim said. "They used to hang horse thieves."

"I tell ya, they don't belong to nobody!"

"Of course they belong to someone." Brynna laughed. "They're wearing brands, aren't they?"

"But they were wild! They just—"

Brynna grabbed Rabbit Eyes's arm before he slugged the younger man. "He's not telling us anything we didn't already know," she said. "So simmer down."

"Things could go a little easier on you," said Jim, "if you tell us where to find the other two gentlemen."

Rabbit Eyes's glare warned the younger man to keep quiet.

"I bet the other guys are worried sick that these

two won't do what they were supposed to do," Brynna teased. "I bet they're waiting at the auction yards right this minute."

"Maybe they are, and maybe they're not," said Rabbit Eyes.

"Here come the rangers to take these tough guys off our hands." Jim watched the approach of another car, but Sam noticed him give Brynna a wink. Without meaning to, Rabbit Eyes had confirmed that there were two other rustlers.

After the rangers and rustlers left, Sam and Brynna spent all morning at the auction yard. They strolled between corrals and trailers, looking for Flick and the freckled man. Sam's eyes burned by the time she and Brynna decided to start for home.

One down and two to go.

Sam tried to celebrate, but she couldn't. She stared out the car window, searching the range as she always did, watching for the Phantom and his band.

A swath of pale green grass covered a hillside, indicating there was water nearby. Water was life to the wild horses, but if she'd noticed it, so would Flick. No horses were safe while Flick was still out there, and Sam couldn't stop worrying.

"I hope you feel good about saving those three mustangs," Brynna said to Sam. "If you hadn't recognized the truck and trailer . . . Well, Jim probably would have sorted out those brands, but who knows?"

Sam nodded, but she kept gazing from the window. She should probably praise Brynna's smooth handling of the rustlers, but Sam didn't want to. She couldn't stop seeing Brynna in Dad's arms the night of the fire. There were plenty of unattached men in Nevada. Let Brynna date one of them.

Apparently, Brynna didn't get the message in Sam's silence.

"By now," Brynna said, "those horses are at Willow Springs with someone looking after them and tossing them flakes of hay."

Sam pictured the horses gobbling hay. Would the mustangs be freed or held for adoption? Would the Phantom miss the two mares and that fine black yearling who reminded Sam of the Phantom at that age?

Would the black grow up to look like his sire? She'd probably never know, but at least now he'd have a chance to grow up.

The trail of grass swept down from the hillside and ended at a red rock wall that looked like crowded-together columns. Nearby, cottonwood trees shaded a dark spot that might be a brook.

Sam couldn't see the water, but the movement of a half dozen mustangs slowly lifting their heads caught her eye.

After that first movement, the horses stood still as the tree trunks. A glint of sun sifted through the cottonwoods and dappled one horse with spots that shone like silver coins. Hidden in the shadows stood the Phantom.

"Stop! Oh, please, Brynna, stop."

Sam didn't want to share this moment, but she couldn't resist. The Phantom and his herd were free, but were they unharmed?

Brynna pulled to the roadside. When Sam started to open the door, Brynna put a hand on her arm.

"Your dad will kill me if I let you approach that stallion."

"I've done it before." Sam heard her own impatience.

"But I didn't give you permission."

"So?" Sam's anger flared. Brynna had no right to give permission or withhold it.

"I *mean*," Brynna corrected herself, "when you got into the Phantom's corral at Willow Springs, you sneaked."

"And we got along fine." Sam held her breath, hoping he wouldn't flee from the strange truck.

Brynna removed her hand from Sam's arm. "I'm not saying go ahead and I'm not watching," she said, but Sam knew she would.

Sam took nothing with her, and she didn't close the truck door. Slow and easy, she walked away from Brynna and the truck. The horses were watching.

In the shade, only one horse moved. Her coat was the color of melted butter. Sam wanted to cheer. Dark Sunshine had found a home with the Phantom.

The buckskin mare was the only horse spooked by Sam's approach. Trying to trot, she split off from the others, but something was terribly wrong.

The mare moved as if her legs were jointless. One leg was so stiff, the buckskin faltered sideways. When she did, Sam saw a red gash marred the mare's chest.

Sam thought of the fire, of Dark Sunshine's screams as she flung herself against the round pen rails, trying to escape. The mare's spirit had been damaged by the rustlers. Now her body was injured, too.

Dad's rules said that every person and animal on the ranch had to earn its keep. She hoped she could get close enough to help Dark Sunshine. If she were lamed beyond help, Dad would write her off as a lost cause.

The Phantom chased after the mare. He charged into the sunlight. Metal-bright glints touched each muscle as he stormed past the buckskin, toward Sam. His legs moved like liquid silver, then blurred and thundered as he came. His head swung from side to side in savage warning.

He didn't know her. Should she run back to the truck?

Sam took a step back, and the stallion slid to a stop. His neck lengthened until he stood taller than ever before. Head level, he drew a breath, and Sam saw his chest swell. His muzzle jerked upward.

*Now he'll know it's me,* she thought. But he didn't.

Pacing like a lion, the stallion moved alongside Dark Sunshine. He shielded her, keeping his body between her and the humans.

*It's me*, Sam wanted to shout. Would anything relieve the ache beneath her breastbone? Only a sign of recognition. *You know I won't hurt her, don't you?*

The stallion caught Sam's scent. His dished Arab head swung to face her and his nostrils quivered. But the Phantom didn't nicker in greeting or come to meet her.

"Then I'll come to you, you stubborn mule," Sam tried to joke, but she heard the quiver in her own voice. The Phantom wasn't acting like her horse.

Brynna sat within easy earshot, so Sam couldn't call out his secret name. Worse, she didn't think it would help.

Right now, he wasn't Zanzibar. He was a wild horse defending his territory. He was a stallion protecting his mate.

Suddenly, he turned. Galloping as if he'd been away too long, the stallion returned to his herd. He stopped just before he reached the cottonwoods and Sam crossed her fingers so hard they hurt.

Now, he'd come back to her. He must. Now.

But the Phantom only stood next to Dark Sunshine, trembling with jealousy.

## *Chapter Seventeen*

BECAUSE GRAM AND DAD had already left to pick up Brynna for Linc Slocum's Brahma-que and Sam was waiting for a ride with Jake, Sam was alone at River Bend when Rachel called.

"Samantha, this is Rachel Slocum."

Sam's mouth opened, but no words came out. Rachel's put-on British accent was thick this afternoon, and unless she'd called to practice it, Sam couldn't imagine why she'd phoned.

They weren't friends and it didn't sound like an emergency. If Rachel hadn't said *Samantha,* Sam would have thought the rich girl had the wrong number.

"Samantha, did we get cut off?" Rachel sounded bored by the possibility.

"Uh, no. I'm here."

"Good, I'm in my bedroom spa and sometimes the telephone reception is not what it should be."

"That's a shame," Sam said. Then another thought popped up. "Aren't you going to your father's party?"

"That's the thing." Rachel sighed. "My father requested that I ask your family to pick up ice on your way over. We're already running short. The caterers are busy serving and the regular hands are doing—cow things."

Sam might have laughed if she hadn't resented taking up the slack for the Slocums' hired help. Of course, there was a good way to view this. If she and Jake stopped in Alkali, they'd spend less time watching Slocum act important.

At the sound of tires crunching in the ranch yard, Sam pulled back the kitchen curtain and saw Jake arrive.

"Samantha, can you do it or not?" Rachel asked. "We'll reimburse you for the expense, of course."

"Sure, Rachel, we can do it," Sam said. "I hope you'll forgive us if we're a little late." She hung up and went to answer Jake's knock.

When Sam opened the door for Jake, she was unprepared for his compliment.

"Hey, you look nice."

"I do?" Sam considered her orange sleeveless top, white shorts, and tennis shoes. She touched her hair, then changed the subject. "How much do you want to go to this Brahma-que?"

Jake shuddered. "More than I want to pump out the septic tank. That was the choice my mom gave me."

"But if your hostess asked you to do a favor on your way to the party," Sam said, "how could you refuse?"

It turned out Jake couldn't refuse, nor could he resist buying two chocolate ice cream cones to pass the time while Clara bagged the ice and loaded it into insulated boxes.

Jake had gobbled his cone and lifted the boxes when Sam's ice cream dripped onto her shorts.

Sam gasped. It was a big blob, and there was no hiding it.

"It figures," Jake said.

"I'll run into Clara's rest room and mop it off. Just go on to the truck. I'll be out in a minute."

The diner's rest room was square and cramped. Because it smelled strongly of cleaning chemicals, a high window was open to the road running behind Clara's and the gas station.

Sam heard a car stop, the crunch of boots on gravel, but she didn't really listen. She didn't have time to go home and change.

*Some people shouldn't wear white*, Sam thought, blotting the spot with a wet paper towel. *And I'm one of them.*

She'd just decided it was looking better when she heard the voice.

"When d'ya think you'll be back?"

Sam stopped. The male voice was so near, it surprised her. It almost sounded familiar.

"Twenty minutes out to Arroyo Azul, maybe an extra five minutes driving back with a load . . ."

Sam recognized the second man. It was Flick.

"That stud's been bringing his herd in at dusk since we scared him out of Lost Canyon."

Flick's voice was low and secretive. She just knew he was talking about the Phantom.

"It doesn't look like I'll get my buckskin back from that kid, but I've got a standing ten-thousand dollar promise for the stallion. Before I leave town, I'm gonna get that dude to make good on it."

Sam's hands were already shaking, but when he added "from that kid," the wet paper towel fell from her fingers to the bathroom floor with a splat.

Did Flick know she'd seen him, or only that she had his horse? No matter, she decided. Arroyo Azul sliced into the mountains next to Lost Canyon. If Flick could get there in twenty minutes, Jake could make it in ten. Nothing mattered except saving the Phantom.

"Go on into Clara's," Flick said, "and have yourself a steak dinner. Meet me here in an hour, and we'll swap the trailer onto the other truck, in case anybody sees me drive from the arroyo.

"And one more thing," Flick added. "She should be at Slocum's, but if that BLM woman shows up, tell her what you're supposed to."

How could Flick know where Brynna was right now? The fact that he did gave Sam chills.

"I'll tell her you've been out of the state for weeks, but I don't think she'll buy it."

"She'll have to," Flick said. "By the time she picks up my trail, it'll be true."

Flick's footsteps had started away when the other man called him back.

"But if something else happens—"

"Lester, there's no trouble Dr. Winchester can't handle."

*Lester and Dr. Winchester.* Sam had more names to give Brynna. If the rangers matched the names with her descriptions, they'd come up with something. But not soon enough.

It was up to her and Jake to save the Phantom.

Sam listened as a truck door slammed, an engine started, tires grated on gravel, and then grew distant. Sam's patience almost snapped as she waited for the second set of boots to walk away. At last, they did.

Sam burst from the rest room and glanced around. She saw no one she knew, except Clara.

"Did you get that ice cream cleaned up, honey?" Clara asked.

Sam had almost forgotten, but her shorts looked pretty good. "Yes, thank you—"

"Big doin's out at the Gold Dust, I hear." Clara paused in wiping down the counter.

"Right," Sam said, shrugging. "Linc Slocum got some new cattle."

Clara chuckled, but Sam didn't stay to joke about

Slocum, no matter how much fun she'd have.

"I'd better hurry and catch Jake before that ice melts."

Sam burst through the door and ran into Jake. He staggered back a step, but she ignored his grunt of surprise.

"You'll never guess what I heard—" Sam stopped, gasping.

"And what might that be?" The man who spoke stood right behind Jake. He had a broad, freckled face she recognized.

It was Lester.

Jake gave him an irritated glance, but Sam thought fast. Giggling, she wrapped her arms around Jake's waist.

"Well, it's sort of private," she whispered, "but I heard you only have to be sixteen to get married in Reno. Isn't that great news, honey?"

Sam hugged Jake with what she hoped was a lovesick expression. Would Lester think she looked sixteen? Would Jake understand her eyes' message: *Don't blow it, Jake?*

"I don't know if that's true." Lester shook his head. "But good luck to you."

Jake nodded his thanks, then swept Sam toward the truck. Sam couldn't walk fast enough to keep up. If Lester had looked back to see what a cute couple they made, he would have seen Jake shoving her along until they reached the truck.

Once inside, Jake began roaring, "What in the —?"

Sam clapped her hand over his mouth, in case Lester was still nearby, but Jake pushed her hand away and kept talking.

"Have you gone completely nuts? Do you want to start the kind of rumors that small town gossips live for?"

"Oh, Jake." Sam closed her eyes and shook her head. "I don't have time for this. That guy"—she stabbed her finger toward Clara's diner—"is one of the rustlers. I heard him talking to Flick."

Sam drew a deep breath as Jake settled down, frowning.

"Flick is on his way to Arroyo Azul to catch the Phantom. *That's* what I was trying to tell you."

"Why didn't you say so, Brat?" Jake nodded toward the road out of town. A feathery trail of dust was scattering on the wind. "That's gotta be him. Let's go."

Convincing Jake they should report Flick had been easy, but they didn't agree on when, so it took most of the drive to hammer out the ground rules of their ambush.

Jake wanted to drive to Slocum's, tell his dad, her dad, and Brynna, then return for a full-scale assault. Sam knew they didn't have time.

Jake wanted to go back to Alkali and phone the county sheriff. Sam knew the sheriff couldn't drive from Darton to Arroyo Azul before Flick escaped.

After twenty minutes of explaining and arguing, Jake declared that what he wanted most was to leave her at the roadside for vultures to peck at.

"Okay, Sam, now listen. This is the last time I'm going to say this," Jake began.

"Drive while you talk," Sam urged.

"I *am* driving!" Jake hit the steering wheel with his palm. "When did you get to be such an expert?"

"I may not be an expert, but I can read a speedometer," Sam insisted. "Every time you turn to yell at me, your speed drops about eight miles per hour."

Then they were back to playing the quiet game. Sam's patience frayed first.

"Let's try this," she said. "We'll go into Arroyo Azul and scare off the horses, then drive like crazy to get help."

As Jake thought about it, they didn't gain on the dust from Flick's truck and trailer, but they didn't fall behind, either.

"What's wrong with that plan?" Sam asked.

"Nothing," Jake said, finally. "But I still don't like it. I don't trust that guy. He hates me and my brothers."

"Oh, Jake," Sam said again.

"Don't 'oh, Jake' me until you've been referred to as 'your kind.' You know, like 'your kind never . . .' or 'your kind always . . .'"

Sam didn't ask what Jake thought Flick meant,

because Jake was driving so fast now that she had to grab the door handle to stay upright.

They were nearing War Drum Flats when Jake pointed.

"When we turn off there, we're committed. He'll know we're after him and I don't know any other way out." Jake looked at Sam with exasperation. She knew he'd be a lot less edgy doing this with one of his brothers. "You still want to do it?"

"Of course."

The truck sped down the road after Flick. Even from this distance, Sam saw the rustler's outline inside the truck. She wondered if he was watching in his rearview mirror. If so, what was he planning to do about them?

"What makes you think he has someone else with him?" Jake asked. "He sure looks alone."

"He's not, though," Sam said. "When Lester asked what Flick would do if there was trouble, Flick said there was no trouble Dr. Winchester couldn't handle."

Jake flinched.

"Gee, Sam," he said. "I sure wish you'd mentioned that earlier. Unless I'm mistaken, that means Flick has brought along a Winchester rifle."

The last climb into Arroyo Azul had to be done on foot. Flick had abandoned his truck at the roadside, but Jake wanted to hide his. He slowed the truck to a crawl, prepared to make a U-turn, and parked behind a stand of juniper.

This was taking way too long and Flick had a head start. Before Jake could stop her, Sam jumped out.

"No, Sam!" Jake shouted.

Sam ran up the path Flick must have taken. She knew this was a little foolhardy, but Jake would be right behind her.

The narrow path ran around the lip of the arroyo. Its steep sides had dozens of narrow rock shelves. She supposed you could reach the turquoise stream below by balancing on one shelf and stepping to another.

Sam felt dizzy as she looked over the edge. From where she stood, she could see Flick's water trap. All he had to do was get down there while the mustangs were drinking and slam the gate.

But Flick was nowhere around. What if he'd taken a shortcut and climbed down to the stream already?

When she looked up at a quick movement across the arroyo, it wasn't Flick she saw, it was the Phantom.

Halfway down to the water, on a rock shelf opposite Sam, the stallion's silver body shone against tawny sandstone. He was watchful, but Sam didn't see any mares down below.

When she'd watched the mustangs come to drink from the pond at War Drum Flats, the stallion had

keep sticking her nose in where it doesn't belong."

Flick touched his upper lip, as if smoothing a mustache that was no longer there. Maybe because he was congratulating himself, Flick didn't hear the little scuff that made Sam think Jake was nearby.

"If you were a little more like Rachel," Flick said to Sam, "you wouldn't get into so much trouble."

"If I were like her," Sam snarled, "I'd want someone to put me out of my misery."

Sam's anger turned to caution. Even though she didn't see Flick's rifle, they were standing on the edge of a cliff. That hadn't been a very smart thing to say.

## Chapter Eighteen ❧

FLICK WAS A RUSTLER, not a killer. Sam tried to remember that.

"I have the buckskin," she said calmly, "but I didn't identify you to the BLM. They saw a bill of sale with your name on it."

"From the bus." Flick's frown said he was kicking himself for not hiding the document better. Then he shrugged. "Don't matter, really, since we're gonna be doin' some horse trading. I know you consider that gray stud yours. So don't worry about the mare. If you ever catch her, we'll be even, horse for horse."

Across the arroyo, the Phantom picked his way down from the rock shelf. Nimble and wary, he found stepping stones to take him lower. His mares were headed into the trap.

"Not much of a deal for you." Flick chuckled. "That buckskin looks about gone."

Dark Sunshine's condition hadn't improved. Stiff

and awkward, she limped along in the middle of the mustang herd. But she was still alive. Sam knew she could help her.

She had to warn them. Sam picked up a rock and threw it.

Flick laughed when the horses didn't pause, then asked, "How'd you know I was comin' here?"

"Lucky guess," Sam said.

"Maybe," Flick said, but the way he watched her had changed. "This is just my lookout, t'see if the horses were in yet. You don't know my shortcut." He gestured toward the bottom of the arroyo.

As he moved closer to her, Sam backed up the trail. She wouldn't let him force her closer to the edge.

"It'll take 'em a while to find you, all trussed up like a calf." Flick touched his leather piggin' strings, "but I don't think you'll die up here."

"She won't." Jake's voice sounded calm and confident, and Sam was very glad to hear it.

Flick stiffened. Because he'd faced Sam as she retreated uphill, his back was to Jake. As Flick turned, he saw what Sam did.

Jake held Flick's rifle.

"If it's not Jake Ely," Flick drawled. "You know, son, that rifle's not loaded."

Jake smiled.

Sam wished her brain would tell her what to do. She wanted to run over there and stand beside Jake.

To do that, though, she'd have to pass within reach of Flick.

"Besides," Flick added, "you're just a kid. You're not going to shoot a man and ruin your life."

Jake's smile got a little harder. "You know what you always say, Flick. There's no telling what *my kind* will do."

Right then, Flick lunged for Jake. Sam tackled Flick's ankles and he went down with a grunt just as Jake threw the rifle over the cliff.

In the arroyo below, mustangs called and galloped, but Sam barely heard them over Flick's cursing. He rolled onto his back, holding his ankle.

"Look what you done! Aw, look what you done to me!"

While Flick was distracted by the pain, Sam darted past.

The instant she was near enough, Jake grabbed her hand and they started running.

"Hurry, Brat." Their feet flew along the path. "Don't fall and don't look back."

"If you'd quit pulling me—"

"No, wait," Flick howled after them. "How'm I supposed to get down? This ankle is swellin' and my boot—"

Jake gave him the same poor sympathy the rustler had given Sam. "It'll take 'em a while to find you," Jake shouted, "but I don't think you'll die up there."

When they reached the foot of the trail, they rushed past Flick's truck and piled into Jake's. Both Jake and Sam were panting like dogs.

"What . . . what if . . . he can walk out before we get back?" Sam managed as Jake started the truck.

"Reach under your seat."

Sam did, and her shaking fingers closed over something metal. "Is this the key to Flick's truck?"

"Yep."

Sam clapped. She bounced up and down. They had him now. Flick couldn't escape before the rangers got here. The horses would be safe.

Sam sighed, weak with relief. Then her sagging eyelids popped open. "Jake, why did you throw that rifle over the cliff?"

She actually heard Jake swallow. He looked more serious than she'd ever seen him before.

"After he threatened to leave you there, I was afraid I might use it," Jake said.

He didn't say another word or take his eyes off the road until they reached the Gold Dust Ranch.

For weeks, folks talked about the stir Jake and Sam created at the Brahma-que. The story of Jake skidding to a stop just short of the life-size ice sculpture of a Brahma bull was told along with one about Brynna, in her lacy blue sundress, searching for her handcuffs before she'd leave her plate of lobster salad. Jen Kenworthy's favorite tale was how she'd

The Phantom had actually charged at her. He didn't love her anymore, and it was all Mikki's fault.

When the white BLM truck pulled up alongside Sam, she wanted to scream.

"Need a lift?" Brynna said through the truck window.

"No, I'm fine."

"Well, I need to give you one," Brynna said. "So, hop in."

Sighing so loudly Brynna couldn't miss it, Sam crossed to the passenger side of the truck and threw her backpack in. As soon as she buckled her seat belt, Sam crossed her arms and stared out the side window.

As usual, Brynna didn't take the hint.

"You're still mad at Mikki, and at me for letting her continue in the program," Brynna said.

It was a dumb, obvious thing to say. Sam tried not to answer, but she couldn't stop herself.

"It's all her fault—the barn, Dark Sunshine's injuries, Phantom hating me—and she barely got punished." Sam sighed again, and turned angrily to look at Brynna.

"Do you know what would happen to me if I was smoking? I'd be grounded for life. And if I burned something down and nearly cost us the barn?"

At a loss to imagine her punishment, Sam shook her head.

"Not grounding, not restriction from television or

The Phantom had actually charged at her. He didn't love her anymore, and it was all Mikki's fault.

When the white BLM truck pulled up alongside Sam, she wanted to scream.

"Need a lift?" Brynna said through the truck window.

"No, I'm fine."

"Well, I need to give you one," Brynna said. "So, hop in."

Sighing so loudly Brynna couldn't miss it, Sam crossed to the passenger side of the truck and threw her backpack in. As soon as she buckled her seat belt, Sam crossed her arms and stared out the side window.

As usual, Brynna didn't take the hint.

"You're still mad at Mikki, and at me for letting her continue in the program," Brynna said.

It was a dumb, obvious thing to say. Sam tried not to answer, but she couldn't stop herself.

"It's all her fault—the barn, Dark Sunshine's injuries, Phantom hating me—and she barely got punished." Sam sighed again, and turned angrily to look at Brynna.

"Do you know what would happen to me if I was smoking? I'd be grounded for life. And if I burned something down and nearly cost us the barn?"

At a loss to imagine her punishment, Sam shook her head.

"Not grounding, not restriction from television or

talking to Jen. I can't even picture what Dad would do to me. And Mikki's off the hook completely."

"Do you think it would be better if I kicked her out of the program? Should I take her out to see Dark Sunshine, and send her home brokenhearted over what she's done?" Brynna asked.

Sam nodded. "Yes, you should."

"I've thought about it," Brynna admitted, "and I don't blame you. But I think I know what would happen if I did."

"What?" Sam wished she hadn't asked, because Brynna braked to a stop just before the River Bend bridge.

"When she got back home, Mikki would paint bitterness over that painful memory, just like she has all the others. She'd forget the good things about working with Popcorn, and she'd keep getting tougher and meaner until it wasn't a coverup anymore. It would be who she really is."

Sam tried to look away from Brynna's serious blue eyes, but her conscience wouldn't let her. Sam remembered her own mistakes. One of them had almost cost Buddy her life. And yet, she'd earned Dad's trust again.

Just as Sam couldn't dismiss Dark Sunshine and the Phantom as lost causes, Brynna wouldn't let her dismiss Mikki. Sam felt her heart open, to give Mikki just one more chance.

❈   ❈   ❈

Mikki's mom had already arrived at the ranch. Her name was Kathy. Kathy's bleached blond hair ballooned away from a thin, nervous face. She chewed gum, hard, as Mikki approached Popcorn in the ten-acre pasture.

Sam leaned against the fence with Dad and Gram while Brynna stood next to Mikki's mom.

"Why are they working here?" Sam asked her father.

"Sort of a test," he said. "It's harder with other horses and plenty of room to run off."

But Popcorn didn't run away. As Mikki walked toward him with the halter and rope, Popcorn quit grazing. Head on high, he trotted toward her.

Sam remembered the rules Jake had set out for Mikki at the very beginning. Popcorn had to come to her without the lure of food. He had to let her touch his face and neck without flinching. He had to trust her. Only then would Jake let her ride the albino.

Popcorn not only tolerated Mikki's touch, he loved it. Sam could tell from the way he pressed his face forward the instant Mikki lifted her hand.

"Yes, he really is a mustang." Brynna was answering a quiet question from Kathy. "He was very badly treated, and Mikki's brought him out of it."

Kathy clapped.

Mikki and Popcorn were startled by the sound.

The gelding sidestepped and his ears showed his discomfort, but he stayed with Mikki, even when she haltered him and Kathy shouted, "You go, honey."

And then the wind blew a message to all ten horses in the pasture. As one, they faced the mountains.

Mikki was leading Popcorn around the pasture when he stopped and nickered.

From the other side of the river, the Phantom trumpeted a challenge. The echo of his summons hung in the afternoon air.

Sam couldn't believe her eyes. The Phantom glowed white and perfect as marble. His mane hung to his shoulder, until he reared, forelegs pawing.

"He's beautiful!"

"Oh, Sam, he's amazing!"

Sam didn't know who spoke. She only knew the Phantom had never before come to River Bend by daylight.

He reared again, neighing for Sam.

She broke into a jog, running to the bridge and trying not to cry.

Dark Sunshine was with him. He nudged the buckskin mare toward the river, but she hesitated in the shallows, afraid to cross without him.

"Come on, girl," Sam called. "You can do it."

The mare wouldn't leave him. She was injured and needed human help. The Phantom seemed to know that, but could he make Dark Sunshine understand?

With a deep, demanding neigh, the Phantom told the mare to stop her nonsense. With a nip, he drove her forward.

Dark Sunshine ran a few faltering steps, then stopped, and suddenly Sam knew what to do.

"Mikki, bring Popcorn." Sam glanced back over her shoulder.

Jake opened the pasture gate. Mikki walked out with Popcorn, but defeat showed in her face.

The last time she'd led Popcorn outside the pen, he'd panicked and she'd failed him. This time she had to be strong. Everything depended on it.

"That's it," Sam encouraged. "Just lead him over the bridge, then down to the water. She knows him. She'll come to him. Then we can help her."

Popcorn stopped at the clumping of his hooves on the wooden bridge. He gave a worried whinny and pranced at the end of the lead rope. Mikki stood still, waiting.

Sam couldn't hear her words, but Mikki spoke to the albino. Her face was nearly as white as his. At last, Popcorn sighed and followed. He left the bridge and walked to the river's edge as if he'd done it every day for years.

Dark Sunshine greeted him with a wild neigh. In a few splashing jumps, she reached the other side and nuzzled his face.

But then the mare turned back, looking at the Phantom, and Sam closed her eyes.

*He let you go to help you. Don't leave.* She turned the bracelet on her wrist, but when she opened her eyes, nothing had changed.

Dark Sunshine still trembled with indecision. The Phantom remained on the wild side of the river. For a full minute, he stood with arched neck and high-flung tail, motionless. Then, feeling all eyes on him, the stallion wheeled.

His muscled haunches propelled him away, tail streaming behind like hundreds of satin ribbons. And then he was gone.

"Lead them back into the pasture, Mikki." Sam's throat hurt, but she got the words out. "Go slowly."

Jake motioned everyone to give Mikki and the horses plenty of room. They did, and the small girl performed like a professional. Even after the pasture gate closed behind her, she stayed calm. With smooth movements, she stroked Popcorn's neck, slipped off his halter, and watched as he and the injured buckskin moved into an awkward run, side by side.

Sam's breath rushed out. She must have been holding it all this time. She heard Brynna's sigh and saw Kathy was crying. As Sam walked past, Dad smiled and Jake gave her a thumbs-up.

The Phantom still trusted her. He'd proven it by bringing Dark Sunshine back. But Sam knew she shared the credit for rescuing Dark Sunshine with Mikki.

When Mikki came back through the pasture gate, she leaned against it with *her* eyes closed. She'd been through a lot.

Sam's fingers went to her bracelet. She slid it off, then held it so the setting sun struck the braid made of many shades of silver.

Sam closed her hand around it one last time and then she extended it to Mikki.

"Why don't you take this home with you," Sam said.

Mikki tucked her hands behind her back. "I can't do that."

"Sure you can. It's not magical, of course, but—" Sam shrugged. "It stands for something."

Mikki nodded. With shaking fingers, she took the bracelet and eased it over her wrist.

A stiff wind blew the scent of grass and horses and leaves turning harvest gold. Popcorn finished his run with the buckskin. He nickered and walked back toward the fence, and Mikki.

"I'll take really good care of it," Mikki promised.

"That's good," Sam said. "Maybe you can wear it when you come back next summer."

"I will," Mikki promised. "If you're sure."

Sam smiled. Mikki was giving her one last chance to take the bracelet back.

"I'm sure," Sam said, but she wasn't looking at Mikki. She was watching the Phantom float ever higher up a trail to the Calico Mountains. "I think I can make another."

From
# Phantom Stallion
## ✑ 4 ✑
## THE RENEGADE

Sam heard the thunder of the Phantom's hooves. She was getting closer. She had to get into the arena before he hurt someone. What if he'd already trampled the man on the ground?

The smell of animals and manure told her she was getting closer. And still no one had followed.

All at once, Sam saw why.

A Brahma bull filled the space between the fences so completely, he couldn't turn. But he knew she was there. He bucked up, looking over the hump of flesh on his back to fix Sam with a glare.

"Maniac!" Sam gasped, transfixed by the mask of black and orange stripes on the bull's face.

She didn't have time to think what it meant, that Linc Slocum's bull was here. But so was Karla Starr. So was the Phantom. It all fit together somehow.

Maniac uttered a rumbling protest. Did he think she was attacking him from behind? Whatever the massive bull thought, he was furious. He loomed over her, coming fast as a truck in reverse, intent on running her down.

From

# Phantom Stallion

### ✎ 4 ✐

## THE RENEGADE

Sam heard the thunder of the Phantom's hooves.
She was getting closer. She had to get into the arena
before he hurt someone. What if he'd already trampled the man on the ground?

The smell of animals and manure told her she was
getting closer. And still no one had followed.

All at once, Sam saw why.

A Brahma bull filled the space between the fences
so completely, he couldn't turn. But he knew she was
there. He bucked up, looking over the hump of flesh
on his back to fix Sam with a glare.

"Maniac!" Sam gasped, transfixed by the mask of
black and orange stripes on the bull's face.

She didn't have time to think what it meant, that
Linc Slocum's bull was here. But so was Karla Starr.
So was the Phantom. It all fit together somehow.

Maniac uttered a rumbling protest. Did he think she
was attacking him from behind? Whatever the massive
bull thought, he was furious. He loomed over her, coming
fast as a truck in reverse, intent on running her down.

*The Renegade* 231

"It's okay, boy," Sam shouted. "It's okay."

Conversation wasn't going to work. He had no reason to think a human meant him well, she guessed, so Sam jumped for her way out.

Her fingers locked on a metal fence rail, then she pulled herself up, hand over hand, tennis shoes searching for each foothold. Maniac backed past her. She knew by the warm blast of breath and the splatter of moisture on the back of her favorite red blouse.

Over the top. Sam sprinted across the next narrow chute, over one more fence, and slid down the wall into the arena.

The Phantom saw her at once. The nervous pacing that had taken him around and around the arena stopped. He was still for only a minute, and then he rushed across the arena.

Sam heard gasps from the grandstands, and shouts summoning help, but she watched her horse. He galloped, head swinging from side to side, then lowered in a snaking, herding motion.

The Phantom stopped about six feet from her, and though every proud line of his body told Sam it was him, something was wrong. The stallion's head cocked to one side, then raised, eyes rolling, as if he couldn't see her clearly. Every sign of horse language she'd learned to read was scrambled.

More commotion rustled through the grandstands as the stallion arched his neck and pranced a circle around her. Some people caught their breath with awe.

A few even clapped, thinking this was a performance.

In a way it was, but Sam turned, always facing the stallion, because she knew what came next. She'd seen this ritual both times the Phantom had fought Hammer.

There. A front leg struck out in challenge, and then he charged. Sam didn't close her eyes. He passed within inches, head swinging out as if to bite, and the metal muzzle struck Sam's shoulder. She felt impact, no pain, and a fierce stab of shame that the stallion might have bitten her if he could have.

The Phantom ran past, and from the corner of her eye, Sam saw a pickup man on a big dun horse, poised to help. Sam swallowed hard.

The Phantom pivoted and walked back. He looked more calm and he talked to her in a low, rumbling nicker, but his eyes still rolled, showing white around the brown.

Sam's world shrank to just this moment, just this horse. Everything depended on her skill at understanding him.

The stallion's forelegs braced apart and his head hung, mane falling forward, forelock covering his eyes. Sam made a quiet smooching and he staggered forward a step.

Inside the metal muzzle, the stallion's velvety lips moved. He lifted his head as if he might have nuzzled her if he could.

"Zanzibar, boy, what have they done to you?"